"What happened on that studio lot that made me run for my life?"

Tears welled in Becca's eyes. "Oh, Zeke, what if I've done something wrong? I told you about the blood on the carpet. What did I do? Did I cause someone harm?"

"Do not think such thoughts."

"Look." She pointed to where broken twigs and trampled underbrush curved left. "This is where I left the path. We need to follow that trail."

Zeke took her hand. "Not tonight. It is late. We can come back tomorrow."

She shivered.

"You are cold. Let me help you into the buggy. Wrap yourself in the blanket. The road is not far."

As Zeke urged the mare forward, Becca glanced back to the fork in the trail. She would come back tomorrow. She had to know more about where she had been that first night. The torn fabric from her dress confirmed her presence.

What else would she find on the trail?

A section of bloodstained carpet? A knife?

She shivered again.

Or a dead body?

Debby Giusti is an award-winning Christian author who met and married her military husband at Fort Knox, Kentucky. Together they traveled the world, raised three wonderful children and have now settled in Atlanta, Georgia, where Debby spins tales of mystery and suspense that touch the heart and soul. Visit Debby online at debbygiusti.com, blog with her at seekerville.blogspot.com and craftieladiesofromance.blogspot.com, and email her at Debby@DebbyGiusti.com.

Visit the Author Profile page at Harlequin.com for more titles.

HER FORGOTTEN AMISH PAST

DEBBY GIUSTI

⬡ **HARLEQUIN**® LOVE INSPIRED® SUSPENSE

Recycling programs
for this product may
not exist in your area.

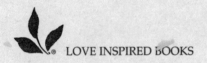

LOVE INSPIRED BOOKS

ISBN-13: 978-1-335-23245-8

Her Forgotten Amish Past

www.Harlequin.com

Printed in U.S.A.

Hear me when I call, O God of my righteousness:
thou hast enlarged me when I was in distress;
have mercy upon me, and hear my prayer.
–Psalm 4:1

In memory of

Betty Ramsdell
August 23, 1919–April 1, 2019

A faithful Christian, devoted army wife
and dear friend.

Thank you, Betty, for your love and support.

ONE

"Hello?"

Becky Taylor tapped on the door of the trailer, then glanced at the Montcliff Studio van parked nearby and raised her voice to be heard over the cold wind that whistled through the tall pines.

"Is anyone there?"

Disheartened to have her knock go unanswered, she pulled her black cape tight around her shoulders and adjusted the starched white *kapp* that covered her knot of unruly hair.

An Amish woman should be able to twist her mane into a smooth and compliant bun, her grandmother's voice from the past challenged. Instead, Becky battled the wayward wisps that danced in the swirling wind. Raking the chestnut strands away from her face, she glanced up at the dark clouds crowding the sky and the descending twilight that brought with it the smell of November rain and musky, red Georgia clay.

Concerned about the encroaching storm, she knocked again, then shrugged and dropped her hand to the knob that turned too easily. Needing to escape the fat drops of rain that, at that moment, started to fall, she stepped into the small entry space, fully intending to make her presence known. The sound of raised voices from a back room made her swallow down the greeting that had almost escaped her lips. Realizing she had overstepped her bounds by entering uninvited, she reached for the door again.

Footsteps sounded behind her. She started to turn, but just that fast, something cold and hard slammed against the side of her head. A scream lodged in her throat.

Pain, like white lightning, exploded across her forehead and ricocheted down her spine. She gasped for air and crumpled to the floor in a swirl of confusion.

A roar filled her ears as she floated in and out of consciousness. The sounds of a struggle followed by a woman's scream. Had she screamed? Someone lifted her hand, wrapped her fingers around a hard object and lowered her arm to the floor again. All the while, she remained dazed by pain and unable to move.

She drifted into a numbing darkness, then jerked awake at the sound of running water as if a person was washing in a sink. She blinked to get her bearings. Her head pounded, and a cloying smell filled her nostrils and made her stomach roll.

Air. She needed fresh air.

Rising to her knees, she reached for the door and hoisted herself upright. An object dropped onto the rug. She glanced down, seeing the knife someone had placed in her hand. Her heart stopped as she stared for a long moment at the trellis-print carpet and the blood.

The room shifted. Fearing she would be sick, she opened the door and stumbled down the steps, needing to get away, away from the blood and the knife and whatever had happened that she couldn't remember.

The rain had stopped, but the ground was wet and her feet slipped on the soggy grass. She staggered toward the dense stand of tall pine trees and hardwoods that edged the property. Her breath clouded the frosty air, and a pounding in her temple kept time with the rapid beating of her heart.

She glanced back and gasped. A man stood backlit in the doorway. Without seeing his face, she felt his gaze and knew instinctively when he spotted her in the descending nightfall. He shouted something, then leaped forward, like a wild animal lunging for its prey.

Run!

She pushed through the underbrush. Tripping on a gnarly root, she caught herself, then lumbered on. Fear compressed her chest, and her lungs burned like fire, but she had to keep moving.

From somewhere behind her, she heard a voice, calling for her to stop. She ignored the warning and pushed on. Bramble and briars tugged at the hem of her dress, catching the fabric and scratching her legs.

Her *kapp* nearly slipped from her head. She grabbed for the ties, hanging unknotted at her neck and glanced back. The sound of him thrashing through the underbrush made her heart pound all the faster.

She could hear his raspy intake of breath. He called out again, but the roar in her ears prevented her from understanding what he said. All she knew was that he was close behind her. Too close.

If she could hear him, he could hear her.

She turned off the path and pushed deeper into the brush. Her foot snagged on a root. She tumbled to the ground, landed on her hands and quickly climbed to her feet. She had to keep moving.

Branches scraped her arms and caught at her cape. She raised her hands to protect her face as she continued on, afraid to stop, fearing what he would do if he found her.

The terrain angled downward. She heard the surge of water and narrowed her gaze in hopes of seeing what lay at the bottom of the steep ravine. As if on cue, the dark clouds parted ever so slightly and a thread of moonlight shone over a rushing waterfall, swollen from the recent rain. Its beauty lost on her, she saw only the steep incline that needed to be navigated if she wished to escape. Far below, the falling water rushed into a cascading river that surged down the mountain.

Glancing over her shoulder again, she searched for her assailant, then turned back too quickly. Her feet slipped out from under her on the rain-slick slope. She screamed as the mountain gave way, sending her tumbling, head over heels down the incline. Rocks scraped and cut her flesh as she somersaulted, over and over again until she came to a stop on a small outlay of soggy soil.

Her shoulder hit the ground and her head crashed against a jagged boulder. Pain seared through her body. She couldn't see or feel or think of anything that had happened. All she knew was that the darkness surrounded her like the dead of night.

Movement on the roadway ahead caught Ezekiel Hochstetler's attention. He pulled back on the reins of his buggy and leaned forward, squinting into the darkness. His mare, Sophie, slowed to a walk and snorted, as if she too wondered what was undulating across the pavement. Surely not a bear. The creature was too slender.

Whatever it was stumbled and swayed as if drunk with muscadine wine or sick with fever.

The buggy drew closer and the moon broke through the clouds covering the night sky. Ezekiel's heart lurched as he spied the calf-length dress and flowing hair.

An Amish woman with her back to him. Was she sick?

Whether sick, or confused and disoriented, one thing was certain, she needed help.

Pulling the buggy to a stop, he hopped to the pavement and slowly approached her. "Ma'am?"

She glanced over her shoulder as if unaware of his approach. Fear flashed from her eyes.

"No," she cried, her voice little more than a whisper.

Turning as if to flee, her feet tangled, one upon the other. She gasped, splayed her arms and started to fall.

He caught her, pulled her close and held her tight as she whimpered and fought to free herself from his grasp.

"I will not harm you," he said, hoping to ease her concern. "You are safe with me."

She struggled, but her feeble attempts were little match for his firm, but gentle hold.

Staring down at her, his gut tightened, seeing the scrapes and cuts on her arms and cheeks. Brambles nested in her hair. Her *kapp* hung to one side of her head, held in place by a crisscross of hairpins. Streaks of blood stood out against the starched white fabric.

What had happened to this woman?

With a last surge of determination, she tried to pull

free, and then her knees buckled and her eyes fluttered closed. She collapsed limp against his chest.

He lifted her into his arms and continued to hold her as he climbed into his buggy and flicked the reins. He could not leave her on the road, not in this condition. He would take her to Hattie's farm. His aunt would provide comfort for the woman and provide for her immediate needs. Water and nourishment, along with salve and bandages to cover her wounds.

Holding her close, Ezekiel was reassured by her breath that played across his neck. Although grateful she was alive, he shook his head in bewilderment. Why would a woman stagger along this desolate stretch of mountain road, far from town or any of the Amish farms that dotted the valley?

Another thought came to mind, but he shoved it aside. He could not dwell on the past. He had moved beyond the pain of Irene's death. At least, he thought he had. Yet something about this woman and the fear he had seen in her eyes brought back all that had happened.

Irene had left him shortly before their wedding, saying she needed time to experience life before she joined the Amish faith and married him. A few weeks later, he had followed after her, hoping to convince her to come back to Amish Mountain. He never suspected Irene had gotten involved with a drug dealer who cooked up methamphetamines in his cabin. Or that she had started using crystal meth.

He shuddered at the memories that welled up unbidden and glanced again at the battered woman in his arms. He needed to focus on her problems and not his own.

Hattie's farm was not far, and the mare covered the

distance at a sprightly trot. Zeke barely touched the reins before Sophie turned into the entrance drive, eager for the oats and hay that awaited her.

Zeke pulled the mare to a stop at the back porch of his aunt's home. Carefully, he climbed down, still holding the bedraggled woman close.

The kitchen door opened, and his aunt stepped onto the porch, her gaze drawn with worry.

"You are late in coming from town, Ezekiel."

As he approached the door, her eyes widened. "What have you brought?"

"A woman, Hattie. I found her wandering on the road."

"She has fainted, *yah*?"

"I fear her condition is far more serious."

Hattie held the door open. "Hurry her into the house and upstairs to the guest room."

Grabbing an oil lamp, his aunt followed him to the second floor and into the bedroom. She pulled back the quilt that covered the bed and stepped aside as he placed the injured woman on the fresh sheet that had dried in the sun and smelled of the outdoors.

Hattie removed the woman's *kapp* and pointed to the streaks of blood, then glanced up at Ezekiel who shared her concern.

"Someone has hurt her," he whispered.

His aunt nodded.

She slipped the black cape from the woman's shoulders and gasped. Zeke's gut twisted, seeing the blood that stained the front of her dress. More blood than would have come from her head wound alone.

"*Gott* help you, Zeke," his aunt said with a shake of her head. "Trouble has found you again."

Thoughts of the explosion and subsequent fire flooded over him again. He had carried Irene from the drug dealer's cabin and had tried to resuscitate her. The memory of her limp body brought the pain back anew.

Giving his heart to an *Englisch* woman over two years ago had been his first mistake. He had made so many, but he was wiser now and would not be swayed by a new pretty face, even if she was Amish.

For the last twenty-four months, he had found solace helping his aunt with the upkeep of her farm. Here in this idyllic mountain setting, he had holed up away from the world. He would not let anyone, even a woman in distress, disrupt his status quo and the tranquil existence he had created for himself.

He sighed at his own foolishness, letting out a lungful of air. The stranger had already thrown his peaceful life into confusion.

TWO

The man was behind her. She heard his footfalls and his grunts and groans as he moved through the underbrush. Her heart pounded nearly out of her chest. She needed to run, but her legs were weighted down and wouldn't move.

She thrashed, trying to escape whatever held her back.

A scream tore through the night.

Hands grabbed her. She fought to free herself.

"No!" she cried.

"Wake up, dear. You are all right. No one will hurt you."

A woman's voice. Not the man who ran after her. She thrashed again.

A soft hand touched her cheek. "You need water. Sit up, dear, and drink."

Water?

She blinked her eyes open to see an older woman with a warm gaze and raised brow.

An oil lamp sat on a side table, casting the small room in shadow.

"My name is Hattie. My nephew brought you here earlier this evening."

"Nephew?" Had he been the man chasing her?

"Ezekiel found you wandering on one of the back roads. You collapsed. He was worried about your health and brought you home."

"I'm… I'm grateful."

"You must tell me your name so we can notify your family tomorrow. I am sure they are worried."

"My name?"

The older woman nodded. "Yes, dear."

"Ah…" Her mind was blank. She rubbed her hand over her forehead. "I'm not sure."

The Amish woman stared down at her for a long moment, then offered a weak smile. "We will not worry about your name now. You can let me know when you do remember."

She reached for a glass of water on the side table. "Sit up, dear, and take a drink. You are thirsty, *yah*?"

Her mouth was parched, like the desert sand. She raised on one elbow and sipped from the offered glass. The cool water soothed her throat.

"Not too much too fast," Hattie cautioned.

A noise sounded in the hall. The two women turned and looked at the open doorway where a man stood, holding a lamp.

He was tall, muscular and clean-shaven with a tangled mass of black hair that fell to his neck.

"Do you need help, Hattie?"

His voice was deep and caused her heart to pound all the more quickly.

"My nephew Ezekiel who brought you here," Hattie explained as an introduction.

She peered around the older woman, trying to see him more clearly. "Thank—thank you, Zeke."

"If you are hungry, I could get something from the kitchen."

"Maybe later."

Hattie patted her hand. "Dawn will come soon enough. Rest now, child. I will wake you for breakfast."

She nodded and glanced again at the doorway, disappointed to find Ezekiel gone. Had she imagined him? Her mind was playing tricks on her so that she struggled to know what was real and what was not.

Blood. She kept seeing blood.

She took another sip from the offered glass and then reached for the older woman's hand and held it tight.

"Hattie, may I ask you a question?"

"Certainly, dear."

She hesitated, unsure of what to ask when her mind was in such turmoil. Would Hattie think her foolish or, even worse, insane?

The older woman leaned closer. "You have been through so much. Perhaps the question can wait until morning."

She shook her head, knowing she needed answers now, at this moment, so she could end the confusion that played through her mind.

Hot tears burned her eyes, but she blinked them back and steeled her resolve. No matter what Hattie thought, she had to ask.

"Who…who am I and why can't I remember my name?"

Zeke had not been able to sleep, not when a strange woman was in the house, a woman who Hattie said did not know her own name. He paced back and forth across the kitchen and then accepted the cup of coffee his aunt offered once the pot had finished brewing.

"Instead of drinking coffee, Ezekiel, you should return to bed. Dawn will not find us for another few hours and there is nothing either of us can do until then."

He glanced down at the sweet woman who had provided not only a home but also acceptance when he needed it most. "I do not see you following your own advice, Hattie."

She chuckled. "Which means both of us are either *dummkopfs* or concerned about our guest."

"You are not a stupid person, although some have called me worse names. For this reason, we cannot get involved."

Hattie frowned. "What do you suggest we do? Throw the woman out with the dishwater?"

He leaned against the counter. "I should not have brought her here."

"As if you would abandon a woman on the side of the road in the middle of the night. Do I know more about you, Ezekiel, than you know about yourself?"

"I know that neither you nor I want our lives disturbed."

"Helping a person in need is more important than our peace and quiet."

He nodded. "You are right. Still, I worry."

"You worry because of what happened, but we learn from our mistakes. Some days I fear you learned too well."

"Meaning what?"

"Meaning you hole up on this farm and venture into town late in the evening and take the long way home as if you are afraid to see anyone. You do not go with me to Sunday church or on visits to friends. You have not spoken to your father for over two years."

He glanced through the kitchen window at the darkness outside. "My father is busy being the bishop."

Hattie tugged at his arm. "*Yah*, he is a busy man, but he is still your father."

Zeke met her gaze. "A father who is disappointed with his son."

She tilted her head and leaned closer. "Then perhaps you must earn his respect again. His love is ever present."

"You accepted me, Hattie."

"I am your mother's sister without children of my own. You have always been the son I never had."

"For which I am grateful."

"Your mother's life ended too quickly for both of us. Your father said it was *Gott*'s will, yet I do not believe *Gott* wills us pain."

"Do not let my father hear you say such things. He will have you shunned for going against the *Ordnung*."

"He did not shun you, Ezekiel."

"Only because I was not baptized."

She raised a brow. "Which you could change."

"Then I would be forced to attend services and listen to my father preach. We would both be uncomfortable."

Hattie tsked. "You are headstrong, like your father."

"I am determined, not headstrong."

"Then why are you running from life instead of facing it?"

He stared at her for a long moment, surprised by the truth in her statement. Hattie was right. She did know him better than he knew himself. He finished the coffee and placed the cup in the sink just as footsteps sounded on the stairs.

They both turned to find the woman staring at them. She was dressed in one of Hattie's nightgowns with a robe wrapped around her slender frame. A bruise darkened her cheek and her left eye was swollen almost shut. Bandages covered cuts on her forehead and lower arms where Hattie had tended her wounds.

"I heard voices," she said, her good eye wide with expectation.

Hattie stepped closer. "Dear, I am sorry we woke you."

"You didn't. I tried to sleep, but…" She glanced at the aluminum coffeepot on the back of the stove. "Do I smell coffee?"

"Forgive me." Hattie pulled a cup from the cabinet and filled it with the hot brew, then handed it to the woman without a name.

She took a sip and glanced at Ezekiel. His stomach churned, not from hunger, but from the way her gaze bore into him as if she could see into the deepest recesses of his heart.

"Thank you again, Ezekiel. A man chased me through the woods. I remember falling, then wandering in the dark, afraid and confused. After that, I awoke in your house."

"My aunt's house," he corrected. "Do you remember anything about the man?"

She shook her head. "I heard him call to me, but I never saw his face."

Turning to Hattie, she asked, "You bandaged my cuts in the night?"

"While you were sleeping. Your soiled dress is soaking. I will find clean clothes for you to wear after breakfast."

"Thank you, Hattie. You are both generous and hospitable."

"We are pleased you could join us. Sit, dear, at the table. It is early, but since we are all up, I will prepare breakfast. You are hungry?"

"I don't want to put you out."

"Ezekiel will slice the bread and fetch the butter from outside. The jelly is on the counter. At least, you will have something to eat while I fry ham and eggs."

"The bread will be enough."

"Perhaps for you, dear, but my nephew will need his breakfast, as well."

Never before at a loss for words, Zeke suddenly felt like the odd man at a sewing bee. Quickly, he sliced the bread and then hurried outside to get the jar of butter cooling in the pail of water by the pump. He dried the jar and returned to the kitchen.

Ham sizzled in the frying pan. The pungent aroma filled the kitchen and made his mouth water. He glanced at the woman who watched him wipe his feet on the braided rug by the door. The latest copy of the *Budget* newspaper lay open on the table.

"Your aunt thought reading the paper might trigger my memory," she volunteered. "I seem to have forgotten everything about my past."

"A blow to the head can cause temporary amnesia," he offered.

She gently touched the bandage that wrapped around her head. "Tell me it won't last long."

"I am certain your memory will soon return," he said with assurance.

"And if it doesn't?"

"My mother always said to take each day as it comes."

Her face lit up and she offered a weak smile. "Good advice."

"Have you read anything in the paper that seems familiar?" he asked.

"A few of the more common surnames. Yoder and Zook. Luke Miller caught my eye as well, yet so many Amish have similar names."

"And your own, dear?" Hattie turned from the stove to ask. "Have you remembered your own name?"

The light in the woman's gaze faded. She bit her lip and glanced down at the newsprint as if searching for a clue to her past. Ezekiel sensed her eagerness to uncover something—anything—that would reveal who she was. Surely, she was confused and frustrated and feeling locked in a world where she did not belong.

He had felt the same way when he had been in jail, awaiting his hearing on wrongful death charges and intent to manufacture a controlled substance, not knowing what the future would hold. At least his memory had not failed him, even if it took a good bit of time before his innocence had been believed.

The woman glanced up. "I think it's coming back to me."

"Have you remembered something?" Hattie asked.

"As I think of names. Becca swirls through my mind and won't let go of me."

"Your first name is Becca?" Zeke asked.

"I believe it could be, along with Troyer as a surname."

"Becca Troyer," he repeated.

She looked at Zeke and tried to smile. He thought

again of the woman covered with blood wandering aimlessly alone in the night. Did amnesia provide the excuse she needed to keep her past hidden?

As much as he wanted to believe her, Becca could be a fraud.

He turned and started for the door.

"Where are you going?" Hattie called.

"To feed the livestock."

"Breakfast is almost ready."

"Later." He grabbed his hat off the wall peg, opened the door and stepped into the cold morning air.

We cannot get involved, he had told Hattie earlier.

Whether he wanted to admit it or not, he was already drawn to Becca Troyer.

THREE

After breakfast, Becca helped with the cleanup and then studied the *Budget* over the next few hours, trying to find something that would trigger her memory. Finally, frustrated, she rubbed her forehead and moaned.

Hattie came closer to the table. "What is wrong, dear? You sound frustrated."

"I have a name, but I want to remember my past, yet nothing comes. What is wrong with me?"

"You have been injured. You have taken a bump to your head, and it has caused you to lose your memory. Give it time, dear. Relax and try not to fret."

Hattie went to the window and peered outside. "Ezekiel must be in the far pasture on the other side of the road. I need to sauté onions and peppers and brown some beef for the midday meal before I search for him."

The older woman's brow furrowed as she turned back to the counter.

Becca left the table. "You are busy, Hattie. I can get Ezekiel, if it would help you. The fresh air would be good for me, but I will need something to wear other than this nightgown and robe."

"I have Amish dresses that might be your size, but

they are in the bottom of a trunk that will take time to unpack." Hattie's eyes widened. "But I bought *Englisch* clothing at the thrift shop in town last week."

"Why *Englisch* clothing?"

"For quilt fabric, dear. The colors were subdued and the fabric perfect for a quilt I plan to make. The clothing is folded on a chair in my bedroom. I washed everything. Go to my room and see if you can find something to wear."

Becca smiled. "Is it allowed for an Amish woman to dress in fancy clothing?"

Hattie smiled. "The dresses are plain. You should find something to wear. By the time you are back from the pasture I will have at least one of the Amish dresses hanging in your room. You can change as soon as you return to the house."

Grateful for the help Hattie had provided, Becca hurried upstairs and found the pile of clothing. Sorting through the dresses, she selected a simple tan dress that looked like it would fit. Although it was a bit shorter than what the Amish usually wore, she was thankful to have clothing and found a lightweight cotton jacket that would provide warmth when she ventured outside.

Hattie smiled her approval as Becca entered the kitchen wearing the secondhand clothing. "Take the water jug on the counter. The paper bag contains two rolls with butter and jelly. Tell Zeke to eat the morning snack now and to come home in a couple hours or so for our midday meal. He is a hard worker and sometimes forgets to eat."

"When did he start working on your farm, Hattie?"

"Two years ago. He had gone through a hard time and needed a place to live away from townspeople who sometimes seem more interested in other people's business rather than their own."

"Zeke helps you," Becca said, "while you help him."

"We are good for each other, *yah*?"

Becca nodded. *"Yah."*

Grabbing the jug and paper bag, she stepped outside and breathed in the fresh mountain air. The day was cold but the sun was bright, which filled her with optimism. As Hattie had mentioned, her memory would return.

Hattie had pointed her in the right direction, and Becca walked along the road and hurried toward the pasture, all the while enjoying the beauty of the crisp fall morning.

In the distance, she saw Ezekiel sinking fence posts. Even from this far away, she could tell his strength by the ease with which he lifted the heavy posts and sunk them into the newly dug holes. For a moment, she almost forgot her own plight.

But that moment passed with the sound of a car engine.

Looking over her shoulder, she saw a black automobile heading down the mountain. Something about the vehicle made her pulse pick up a notch, or maybe it was being alone on the deserted mountain road that caused her to be anxious. She crossed the road, glanced at the pasture, and then studied the forest that surrounded it, hoping the trees and underbrush would provide enough cover if she needed to hide.

Her pulse accelerated as the car increased its speed.

The pasture where Ezekiel worked sat far from the road. He had his back to her and was probably unable to hear the vehicle. No doubt, he was focused on his work and oblivious to what she was beginning to believe was an encroaching risk.

Reacting to her gut instinct, she made her way into the wooded area and stepped behind a large boulder. Crouching down, she watched the car draw closer. She was probably overreacting, but after last night it would behoove her to be careful.

Relieved when the vehicle passed by, she started back toward the road but, once again, heard the sound of a car's engine. Glancing in the direction the black car had gone, she realized it had turned around and was coming back.

She returned to the boulder and hunkered down once again. This time her heart pounded even more rapidly.

The car pulled to the side of the road and a man exited from the driver's side. Early thirties with brown hair pulled into a man bun and a full beard. He had broad shoulders, stood well over six feet tall, and was wearing jeans and a pullover fleece.

He stepped away from the car and peered into the woods, his gaze homing in on the boulder where she hid. Her chest tightened and everything within her cried danger.

Not that she needed a warning. The man's scowl was enough to cause a wad of fear to jam her throat.

He took a few steps forward and stopped again to study the area. Her heart pounded so hard, she was sure he could hear its erratic cadence.

Glancing over her shoulder, she spied a cluster of large rocks farther from the roadway. Slowly and carefully, she scurried toward the hiding spot and stopped on the far side to catch her breath. She placed the water jug and rolls on the ground and peered around the boulder, relieved to find him still staring into the distance.

Leaving the bag and water behind, she again retreated, going farther into the woods.

A twig snapped. She glanced back, fearful.

He stared in her direction, then started running.

She raced deeper into the woods, leaping over downed trees and skirting low patches of underbrush. The branches and brambles tugged at her dress and scraped her already raw hands and legs. Her side ached and her head pounded.

She glanced back, hearing him trample through the underbrush and hoping he couldn't hear her footfalls over the noise he was making.

Ezekiel continued to focus on the fence. She yearned for him to glance up and notice the man who had picked up his pace and seemed to be running directly toward her.

She caught her next breath, then ran to the pasture. She could see Zeke at the far end of the cleared area, still intent on his work. She waved her hand, hoping he would see her.

The gate to the pasture lay ahead. She heard the man behind her. Trembling with fear, she struggled with the latch, pushed open the gate and sprinted forward.

A snort sounded to her left. She glanced in that direction and came to an abrupt halt. A huge bull stood staring at her.

From some place deep inside her, a warning bubbled up. She did an about-face and rapidly retraced her steps. Without taking time to shut the gate, she turned right and ran toward another cluster of boulders. Collapsing against the rocks, she drew in a breath and watched the man race through the open gate, into the pasture, oblivious to the danger.

The bull charged.

The man turned around, rapidly retraced his steps and slammed the gate closed barely in time to stop the angry bull. Heaving for air, her pursuer glanced around, no doubt searching for her, then staggered back to his car.

Becca rested her head against the boulder. Tears of relief stung her eyes. She wiped them away, needing to be strong, and turned her attention back to the pasture.

Ezekiel must have seen what had happened because he was running along the outside of the pasture. The bull charged the fence. Big as he was, Becca wasn't sure the wood barrier would hold.

She hurried forward, slipped out of her jacket and waved it in the air. Her distraction worked. The massive animal eyed Becca, then made his way back to the center of the pasture.

Zeke rounded the fence and ran to where she stood. He grabbed her hand, and both of them raced behind the boulder and hid.

A motor sounded. Through the trees, they saw the black sedan drive away.

"Was that the man who chased you last night?" Zeke asked.

"I never saw the man's face last night so I'm not sure."

Becca's head pounded. If he wasn't the guy from last night, then two men had chased after her in less than twenty-four hours.

As they watched, the man pulled into Hattie's drive as if to turn around. He climbed from his car, hurried to the porch and pounded on the door.

"Oh, Zeke." Becca grabbed his hand. "That man is crazy."

Zeke pointed to the henhouse where his aunt peered from a window. "Hattie is gathering eggs. Hopefully, she stays put and doesn't try to engage the man."

He pounded on the door again, then turned to stare at the farm. Evidently he thought no one was home because he returned to the car and headed down the mountain toward town.

Both Zeke and Becca let out huge breaths of relief once he had driven away. "Let's hurry back to the house. I want to warn Hattie to get inside in case that guy returns."

"I'm so sorry, Zeke."

"You did not cause the man to chase after you."

"But I've caused so many problems."

He smiled, seeing her worry. "You are not the problem, Becca. The man is."

After retrieving the water jug and bag Becca had discarded, they crossed the road and hurried to the house. Hattie met them on the porch and filled them in on the unexpected visitor. Becca and Zeke shared their own plight and their concern for Hattie's safety.

Once inside, Becca went upstairs to change into the Amish dress Hattie had hung in the guest room.

"This man worries me." His aunt gave Zeke a troubling glance as she washed her hands and dried them on a towel. "The man sees Becca walking along the road dressed like the *Englisch* and starts running after her. I may be getting old, but my mind is still sharp, yet I do not understand what this means."

"It means Becca needs to be careful and so do you. Do not open the door if the man returns."

Her eyes widened. "You think we will see him again?"

"I do not know, but we will take precautions, *yah*?"

"I am grateful you are with me here on the mountain, Ezekiel. My worry would be even greater if I were living alone."

"Soon Becca's memory will return. Then we will know her story and who was running after her."

Zeke left the house and headed to the barn. The mountain had been peaceful before Becca had appeared in the middle of the night. As he had told her, she was not to blame for upsetting their peaceful existence, yet she had to be involved in something outside the norm since a man was so desperate to find her. Or had two different men chased after her?

He glanced up at the guest room window, thinking of her pretty eyes and smooth skin. Zeke wanted to know the truth about the stranger who was staying with them.

A question kept troubling him. Who had chased after her and why?

FOUR

The sun was high in the sky by the time Ezekiel finished the chores. He wiped his brow, thankful for the cool mountain breeze and glanced at the blue sky, wishing life could be as clear.

Yesterday morn he had worried about the price of corn and soybeans. Today was filled with thoughts of the woman he had found last night.

Since then, he had been in an emotional tug-of-war. His intellect cautioned him to be careful, whereas his heart wanted to trust the woman without a past.

Amnesia or prevarication?

Irene had lied to him all the while she had worked her way into his heart until he was unable to think clearly. *Besotted*, his father had called him. The fact that Irene's father and her brother, Caleb, had left the Amish faith only added to his own *datt*'s irritation about Zeke's choice of women.

Amish men only marry Amish women, his father had told him on more than one occasion, yet his father did not know Irene or what she had shared with Ezekiel.

I want to return to the Amish way with you, Zeke, Irene had assured him, *after I see the world.*

The world she explored had been the small town of Petersville, known for illegal activity and a police department that turned a blind eye to crime.

The kitchen door opened, and Becca stepped onto the porch. Ezekiel's throat tightened, recognizing the pale blue dress she wore. A wedding dress Hattie had made for Irene, the woman Zeke had planned to marry.

"Hattie said lunch is almost ready. You didn't eat breakfast so you must be hungry."

He had been hungry, but after seeing Irene's dress, his appetite left him. "I will join you soon."

Becca hugged her arms as if chilled by the mountain air. "Your aunt found this dress for me to wear until mine is washed and dried."

Once again he was at a loss for words. The woman needed clothing, other than the *Englisch* clothing from the thrift shop, and Hattie had solved that need. Why had her generosity unsettled him?

"Is something wrong?" Becca asked.

"No, of course not." But something was wrong. His quiet life had been turned upside down.

She stared at him for a long moment as if wanting to say something more, then with a nod, she turned and entered the house.

He let out an exasperated sigh. How could life become so convoluted overnight? He rolled up his sleeves and washed his hands at the pump and dried them on the towel. In the distance, higher up the mountain, three buzzards circled in the morning sky. He paused to watch their flight, then turned at the sound of a car coming down the mountain, a flashy sports car, traveling too fast over the narrow road.

He recognized the man at the wheel and waited until

Caleb Gingerich, Irene's brother, braked to a stop. Tall, gangly and midtwenties, Caleb climbed from the cherry red convertible and extended his hand. "Good to see you, Zeke."

Hattie left the kitchen and stepped onto the porch.

"What brings you to this side of the mountain?" Zeke asked, irritation evident in his voice.

Caleb chuckled. "A piece of Hattie's pie."

Zeke glanced at his aunt. "She has not baked today."

On any other day, Hattie would insist on setting another plate at the table for anyone passing by, but this was not any other day, not with their mysterious newcomer inside.

No doubt hearing the frustration in Zeke's voice, the younger man's smile vanished. "After my sister's death, didn't we talk about moving beyond that which divides our families?"

"As I recall, you did the talking, Caleb. Besides, your father will never change."

"He grieves for Irene, but I thought we could move beyond the past. I forgave you."

Zeke's gut tightened. "There was nothing to forgive, no matter what your father says."

Seemingly exasperated by Zeke's response, the younger man turned toward the porch. "Expect someone from the movie studio to stop by, Ms. Hattie."

"A bearded guy?" Zeke asked, thinking of the man from this morning.

"A tall guy, clean-shaven," Caleb said. "The studio needs an Amish farm on which to film a trailer for their next movie, and I mentioned your land. They pay well."

"Is that how you bought your new sports car?" Zeke asked, his tone sharp.

"Credit, Zeke. Something you Amish don't understand."

"It was not that long ago when you and your family were Amish."

"Things change."

Ezekiel knew that all too well.

Hattie hurried down the steps and walked to where the two men stood. "I still do not understand why a movie studio comes to Amish Mountain."

"For the idyllic setting." Caleb spread his hands and peered at the surrounding area. "Plus Georgia is considered the Hollywood of the South."

She shook her head with frustration. "Hollywood needs to stay in California."

Glancing at the convertible, she added, "You must be careful, Caleb. Driving so fast on the winding roads is dangerous."

He laughed. "Tell that to Zeke. There are more buggy accidents than automobile crashes on Amish Mountain. I bought the car because I'm working at the studio now."

Hattie raised her brow. "You are a movie star?"

"Maybe someday. Right now, I'm working in the commissary. You should stop by sometime. I could show you around."

"Commissary?" she asked.

"The dining hall where the crew eats," Caleb explained.

"They are filming there now?"

"For the next few days, they're shooting some extra scenes in town. The leading lady is being a little cantankerous. You know how temperamental movie stars can be."

Something Ezekiel did not know. He doubted his aunt knew anything about Hollywood types either.

"Seems she left the lot," Caleb continued, "and won't answer her cell phone. The director is putting up a good front, but from what I've heard, he's worried."

"Worried she will not return to complete the film?" Hattie asked.

"That's what I understand, although rumor has it she's been difficult since filming began. Some folks thought the director was ready to fire her, but the producer stepped in and insisted the movie wouldn't get the backing it needs without her."

"An actress leaves before the filming ends?" Hattie shook her head. "I do not understand how that could be."

"The ways of the world, Hattie, are not as the Amish live."

"*Ach*, it is so."

"I told Zeke that I stopped by for a slice of pie, but I really wanted to talk about buying some of your eggs. The studio cook who fixes meals for the cast and crew has been going to town for his supplies. I told him you might be able to provide fresh eggs from your chickens. I also mentioned your pies and cakes. He's interested in purchasing your homemade desserts, if you have time for extra baking. You would be paid well for your efforts."

Hattie thought for a moment and then nodded. "*Yah*, this is something I can do."

Zeke touched her arm. "Are you sure you want to get involved with the studio?"

"What could be the harm?" She patted his hand as if to dismiss his concern and then turned to Caleb. "Yesterday, I baked cookies. You will take a dozen to the cook. He can decide if he is interested in buying my baked goods."

Hattie hurried inside and returned with a filled cookie tin that she handed to Caleb. "You will let me know?"

"I'm sure he'll agree to buy anything you can provide." Caleb placed the tin on the passenger seat and rounded the car to the driver's side.

Ezekiel glanced up and spied Becca at the kitchen window. Her expression made his breath catch.

"You mentioned the missing movie star," he said before Caleb climbed behind the wheel. "What does she look like?"

"I've got a picture of her on my phone. She's a nice lady, but evidently a little hard to handle. I downloaded her headshot." He tapped his phone and held it out for Ezekiel to see. "There she is. Vanessa Harrington. You wouldn't forget her if you saw her."

Ezekiel took the phone. Hattie stepped closer and both of them stared at the woman filling the screen. She was attractive with long black hair, big brown eyes, high cheekbones and a mouth that puckered into a half pout, half smile.

Relaxing ever so slightly, Zeke handed the phone back to Caleb. "She looks to be in her thirties," he said, hoping Hattie did not hear the relief in his voice.

"More like midforties, but makeup does wonders." Caleb swiped his finger over his phone and held up a second photo. "Here she is with the producer, Nick Walker, and Kevin Adams, her leading man. The producer's the big guy in the suit. The actor's the bodybuilder with a beard."

Zeke glanced momentarily at the second photo, noticing the younger man's arm around the actress's shoulders. The producer stood behind them, wearing a scowl on his square face.

"The producer does not look happy," Zeke stated the obvious.

Caleb chuckled. "Mr. Walker is not known for his good humor. He and Vanessa spent a lot of time together from what I've heard. Evidently their so-called friendship has cooled somewhat."

"And the younger man has moved in?"

Caleb shrugged. "Who knows? Although gossip at the studio is as plentiful as acorns on an oak tree."

"Has anyone else gone missing from the studio?" Zeke asked.

"Not that I know of." Caleb shoved his phone into his pocket. "Why do you ask?"

"Just wondering. I presume the behind-the-scenes folks in the movie industry change jobs frequently. It is probably hard to get good workers."

"I'm just glad they hired me." Caleb opened the car door and slid behind the wheel. "I'll stop by once I hear from the cook."

As he pulled out of the drive, the kitchen door opened. Becca appeared anxious as she stepped onto the porch. "Did you tell him about me?"

Hattie hurried up the stairs and rubbed her hand over the younger woman's shoulder. "You need not worry, dear. Caleb works at the movie studio nearby. The cook at the studio wants to buy some of my baked goods and eggs. We did not mention you."

Hattie glanced back. "Come inside, Zeke. You need to eat."

His aunt was right. He was hungry.

Climbing the porch steps, Zeke smiled at the new-comer, hoping to ease the tension that lined her pretty face. Her brow was tight with concern as she narrowed her gaze and stepped closer.

"Could there have been an accident on the mountain?" she asked, rubbing her arms as if she was cold.

Which he had not considered. An overturned buggy could be the reason for the blood on the woman's dress and the lump on her head, yet Becca had mentioned being chased through the woods. Could she have been involved in a buggy accident, as well?

Zeke looked again at where the buzzards had flown earlier. Now they were gone. Had they found a carcass and were picking it clean? A horse perhaps?

His gut tightened.

Or something else?

Becca hurried inside and then turned toward the door as Ezekiel followed her into the kitchen. His smile had vanished, and the frown he had worn earlier this morning had returned to darken his gaze.

Hattie stepped to the stove and stirred the hamburger mixed with a sloppy Joe tomato sauce. The scent of the simmering meat filled the kitchen with mouthwatering goodness. She said something to Zeke in a dialect that made no sense.

Just as before, Becca nodded as if she understood and hoped her response was appropriate. She didn't want Hattie or Ezekiel to know she had forgotten how to converse in the language common to the Amish.

Every thought that rumbled through her mind was in English, not German and not Pennsylvania Dutch.

Yet she *was* Amish. Wasn't she?

Evidently, not a very good Amish woman. The plain people were nonviolent, which meant she shouldn't have been running away from someone all the while wearing a dress stained with blood.

Something had happened in the woods. If only she could remember what.

Reaching around Hattie, she grabbed the coffeepot and poured a cup of the hot brew, then offered it to Zeke.

"Danki." He raised the cup to his lips, his eyes never leaving her face. Her cheeks grew warm and a tingle curved around her neck.

Abruptly, he lowered the cup and headed to the table, for which she was grateful. His nearness had unsettled her all the more. She returned the coffeepot to the stove and glanced at the stairway, longing to retreat to the guest bedroom so she wouldn't have to face her handsome rescuer whose mood swings confused her almost as much as her own lack of memory.

"Sit, dear." Hattie motioned her toward the table. "The sloppy Joes are almost ready to serve. You can help me then."

"Has anything new come to you?" Ezekiel asked as she slipped into the chair across from him.

"I have thought of nothing except what I cannot remember," she admitted. "And still I remember nothing."

Glancing down, she added, "I keep thinking of the Troyer family to which I must belong since the name seems so familiar."

She dipped her head. "While you were outside, Hattie placed a wet tea bag on my eye to draw the swelling. As you can see, thanks to her home remedy, it is better."

"Do not thank me, dear. It was the tannin in the tea."

"All the while the tea was working, I thought of the

Troyers and what they must be like. Hattie mentioned a Troyer family living in the valley."

"The wife's name is Ida, dear. She and her husband have five boys." Hattie reached for a plate and heaped the meat mixture onto a bun, then held it out for Becca who hurried to the stove to help. "Serve Ezekiel first."

Zeke nodded his appreciation when Becca placed the plate in front of him.

Hattie handed a second plate to Becca. "It looks *gut, yah*?"

"And smells delicious." Becca stared at the fresh bun overflowing with the juicy mixture. Just as at breakfast, the portions were generous. "You've given me far more than I can eat, Hattie. This should be your plate."

"You ate little this morning, dear. I do not want you going hungry."

"Hattie, no one could go hungry in your house." Zeke chuckled from the table. "You are a bountiful cook."

His aunt seemed to appreciate the remark and said something in reply that Becca could not understand. A look of concern passed over the sweet woman's face before she repeated the statement in English.

"Surely you know the Amish saying, dear. When the man grows the food and the woman cooks the food, both eat to their fill."

Without commenting further on Becca's inability to comprehend the Pennsylvania Dutch dialect, Hattie pointed to the chair across from Ezekiel. "Sit, dear, before the food grows cold."

Taking her place at the table, Becca kept her hands on her lap, unsure of the midday meal routine. This morning she had started to eat and then noticed Hattie bowing her head to give thanks. She didn't want to make the same mistake twice.

Once Hattie was seated, Zeke lowered his gaze. Hattie did the same and Becca followed suit. From the recesses of her limited memory a prayer surfaced.

Thank you for this food and bless all of us today, especially those who cannot be here. Bring peace to our hearts, lighten our steps and help us to do all things according to Your Holy Will. Amen.

She should have been relieved to remember something, anything, but recalling the short prayer only made her want to remember more.

Was it an Amish prayer that she had said with her parents as a child? Or a prayer she said with her own children? How could a mother forget her little ones, those she should love most?

Ezekiel said something.

She glanced up to find him offering an open jar of pickles. She jabbed one with a fork and placed the pickle on her plate. *"Danki."*

Hattie patted her hand. "Is everything all right, dear? You look troubled."

"I'm concerned about upsetting you both by being here."

"Do not think such thoughts. We are happy to have you as our guest."

Becca glanced at Zeke. His eyes were on his plate. He didn't seem as enthusiastic as his aunt about having a stranger in the house, yet he had been the one to bring her here.

She shuddered thinking of what could have happened if he hadn't found her.

"Is that not right, Ezekiel?"

He glanced at his aunt, his brow raised.

"I said that we are both glad to have Becca with us, *yah*?" Hattie prompted.

He turned his dark eyes on her again, making Becca's breath catch as she lost herself for a moment in his gaze. If only she could read his mind.

She reached for her fork. "I am thankful you found me, Ezekiel. If you had not—"

She couldn't go on. Her mind failed to remember the past, yet it could bring forward terrible thoughts of what could have happened last night.

"All things work together for good," Hattie intoned with a definitive nod of her head.

Becca wasn't as sure. She took a bite of the meat mixture, but the food stuck in her throat. More than anything, she wanted to push back from the table and run upstairs to hide from Zeke's dark eyes and all the questions she saw in his troubled gaze.

She didn't want to bother this man and his aunt any longer, but before leaving, she needed to find out who she was, no matter how difficult the truth might be to accept.

"Did I hear you mention a nearby town?" she asked, needing something on which to focus other than the man sitting across the table from her.

"*Yah*, Willkommen," Hattie answered. "It is some miles away. Does the name sound familiar, dear?"

"Regrettably, nothing sounds familiar."

Zeke reached for his coffee cup. "You wish to go there?"

"It might help me remember if something triggers my memory."

"Willkommen has a sheriff," Hattie mused. "He might know of anyone who is missing."

"You mean he might have information regarding who I am and where I live?"

Hattie leaned closer. "*Yah*, but I must warn you, dear. If you go to town and ask questions, you could find more than you want to know."

"I don't understand."

She rubbed Becca's hand. "Think, dear. You were running from someone last night. If you notify the sheriff, he could tell the person who was chasing after you."

Hattie shrugged before adding, "A mean husband is someone to fear."

Becca glanced at Ezekiel, then turned back to Hattie. "I don't feel like I have a husband."

"And how would that feel, dear?"

"I… I'm not sure, but wouldn't I remember the man I loved?"

Hattie leaned even closer. "Perhaps you have a husband you do *not* love."

"Yet if I am married, there could be children."

Ezekiel's gaze darkened all the more. The direction of the conversation seemed to be unsettling to both of them. "I will go to town and see for myself without involving the sheriff," Becca said. "Perhaps then I will remember."

"Ezekiel will take you in the buggy," Hattie volunteered. "But you must dress so no one will recognize you."

"What are you suggesting?"

"You should wear men's clothing, dear. You are slim and not so tall. People would think you a young Amish lad."

Hattie sat back and smiled with satisfaction. "Dressing as a man would be a perfect cover. Ezekiel's clothing is too big for you, but I kept a few of my husband's things. I will find something you can wear."

Ezekiel stared at Becca, as if she had been the one to suggest the idea of dressing as a man. Hattie was right. The costume would keep Becca from being recognized, especially from anyone who might do her harm, yet the idea of needing to hide her identity from others when she didn't even know who she was or where she lived weighed heavy on her shoulders.

The sound of a vehicle turning into the drive made Becca's heart stop. Zeke glanced at her as if he too was concerned.

"Stay here," he cautioned as he rose from the table and walked to the door, grabbing his hat before he stepped outside.

"Ach." Hattie patted her chest as if patting down a swell of apprehension, which was exactly what Becca had bubbling up in her own throat. "I do not know who would be coming to see us."

Hattie's gaze narrowed, and she pursed her lips. Then, with a shrug of her shoulders, she added, "We go for days without visitors and now they come one after the other."

Some friendly and some not, Becca thought, her stomach a jumble of nerves. Didn't Hattie realize they were coming because she was here?

Hattie pushed back from the table, hurried to the sink and then peered from the kitchen window. "It is a tall man who steps from a van. The Montcliff Studio logo is on the passenger door."

She glanced back at Becca. "I will go outside to

learn the purpose of his visit. Perhaps it is the man Caleb mentioned."

"Please, Hattie, don't invite him in."

The older woman nodded, then reached for the door-knob and stepped onto the porch, leaving the door ajar.

In spite of the cool air coming through the open doorway, Becca moved closer, hoping to overhear what was being said. Her pulse raced when she peered out-side. A tall, muscular man stood by the van.

The footfalls of the man who had chased after her last night played through her memory. From the sound of him stomping through the underbrush, he had to have been a big man, tall in stature and with a bulky build.

Her gaze homed in on the Montcliff Studio logo on the side of the van. Apprehension zigzagged along her spine as she stared at the black-and-white graphic, long-ing to remember why it drew her attention.

The man walked to the front of the van, closer to where Zeke stood.

A lump jammed Becca's throat as she saw the movie man's long legs and thick build. Hands on his hips, he stared at the barn and then the outbuildings as if search-ing for something.

Was he searching for her?

Tears burned Becca's eyes, but she forced them back. Why would an *Englisch* man from a movie studio be looking for her?

He extended his hand to Zeke. "The name's Larry Landers. I'm the location manager at Montcliff."

Zeke accepted his handshake without comment.

"The movie studio," Larry added as if for clarifica-tion. "As you probably know, we've been here for the last six months."

"I know about the studio, Mr. Landers," Zeke said. "It is located higher up the mountain on Levi Gingerich's land."

"That's right. We're almost finished with the production of our first film and hope to begin work on our next project in a few weeks. I'm looking for farmland on which to shoot a trailer and a few preliminary scenes, maybe as early as the end of the week."

"An Amish farm?" Zeke seemed perplexed by the statement.

Landers chuckled, although the gruff sound was anything but humorous. "I mentioned shooting, but not with a weapon, if that's what you're thinking."

Raising his hand, palm out, Landers quickly added, "I know you folks are pacifists."

Becca heard disdain in the man's voice.

"What I meant," Landers continued, "was shooting the film. And yes, we're scheduled to shoot an Amish story and are looking for an Amish farm, otherwise we might have to use someplace in town."

He pulled a folder from the van and handed the packet to Zeke. "The studio will pay to use your property for a week or two, depending on the weather. We'll need your authorization. Our landscape crew will arrive as soon as the contract is signed. Their job will be to enhance the property."

"The land is as *Gott* provided, Mr. Landers. It does not need to be enhanced."

"You're right, of course. Be assured you'll be compensated for your time and trouble."

Zeke glanced at the contract, then closed the folder and handed it back. "The farm belongs to my aunt. She is not interested in your contract."

"You didn't read the offer." Landers gazed at the barn and the pasture where the horses grazed. "You folks look like you could use some financial help. I can increase the payment by half to sweeten the deal."

"Sweet or sour, there is no deal, Mr. Landers."

"Look, I apologize if I've upset you. Perhaps if I talked to your aunt."

Noticing Hattie on the porch, he took a step forward. "Ma'am, if I could have a moment of your time."

"You would not hear anything different from her." Zeke's tone was firm.

"What about some of your neighbors?" Landers asked.

"You will find more farms in the valley. Some are owned and operated by *Englisch* farmers. Perhaps they would be willing to rent their land."

The guy shook his head with frustration. "You're missing an excellent opportunity."

Again, he played his gaze over the barn, then turned and stared at the kitchen door for a long moment.

Becca drew back, fearing he could see her. If so, would he recognize her?

He hesitated for a long moment and then added, "Have you folks seen anyone from the movie studio wandering around in the area?"

"Why do you pose such a question?" Zeke asked.

Larry offered a half-hearted smile. "The relationship between the Amish and our studio is not the best. I want to ensure we don't disrupt your way of life more than we already have."

"No one unknown has come through my aunt's property, if that is your question."

The guy glanced once more at the house. Becca's heart stopped. She held her breath, fearing he had seen her.

Abruptly, Landers turned and scanned the rest of the farm.

"Let me know if you change your mind about the land." He shook Zeke's hand, then threw the folder onto the passenger seat and climbed behind the wheel. Without further comment, he backed the van onto the road.

"Levi Gingerich never should have rented his property to those movie people," Hattie groused as she pushed on the kitchen door and wiped her feet on the entry rug. Zeke followed her inside.

"Levi may have needed money," she continued. "But we do not need a movie studio on the mountain. I have seen some of those people in town. They do not understand the Amish way. Plus, from what I have heard, they are a wild bunch who do not conform to Christian values."

"You are lumping them all together into one pot," Zeke cautioned. "I am sure the majority of the actors and actresses are *gut* people."

Hattie harrumphed as she walked past Becca and headed to the stove. Zeke returned to the table without comment.

Becca's heart beat erratically. The tall, muscular man had been looking for someone. Did Zeke and Hattie not realize he could have been looking for her?

She glanced first at Hattie and then back at Zeke. Grateful though she was for their hospitality, she was a stranger in their midst. A stranger with a made-up name and no knowledge of the life she had lived or even her age. A man had chased her last night, and she had been chased again this morning. Now another man with a haughty manner had stopped at the farm.

Tears stung her eyes, but they were a sign of weakness, at least that's what a little voice whispered in her head. A voice from the past perhaps? How could she know what was memory and what was her own mind playing tricks on her?

"Becca, are you all right?" Hattie asked.

"If you don't mind, I need to go to my room." She left the kitchen and climbed the stairs, stepping into the bedroom just as the tears started to fall.

She closed the door behind her and moved to the window, wanting to ensure the studio van was out of sight. Her heart lurched when she saw the vehicle stopped on the side of the mountain road. Larry Landers stood in front of the Montcliff Studio logo on the side of his van. He held binoculars to his eyes and was staring back at Hattie's house.

Becca jerked away from the window. Fear gripped her anew. Her pulse raced. Who was the man from the movie studio and why was he spying on her?

Pulling in a deep breath, she moved closer and peered again from the window. A black car like the one she had seen this morning had pulled behind the studio van and a bearded man with his hair pulled into a bun was talking to Landers.

Was he asking about an *Englisch* woman he had seen walking along the roadway? As she watched, the bearded man turned and stared at Hattie's house, seemingly zeroing in on the guest room window. Again, Becca stepped back, her heart in her throat.

She dropped her head into her hands. The worry and anxiety that had circled through her mind collided in a wave of emotion, like a giant tsunami washing over her. Hot tears ran down her cheeks and dampened her dress, but she couldn't stop their onslaught.

Struggling to remember anything, she thought back to the woods where the branches had caught at her dress. Was Larry Landers the person who had chased after her last night? Or could it have been the bearded man with the bun? If only she could have seen the man's face, but all she could remember was the blood on the carpet. So much blood.

She thought of something else that made her pulse race even more.

The knife.

Her heart stopped.

The knife that had dropped from her hand was covered with blood.

FIVE

"Tuck your hair into this hat," Hattie instructed the next afternoon as she handed a wide-brim black hat to Becca. "My husband's clothing fits you well, *yah*? The hat will sit low on your head and cover your hair. It will also cover the swelling on your head and the bruise on your cheek."

"And what happens if I go inside and need to remove my hat?" Becca asked.

"You will leave it on. A young boy will not be noticed but stay in the buggy if you are concerned. You will see with your eyes as Ezekiel drives through town. Something might bring back your memory. A store, a street, a person. You must be watchful."

Hattie adjusted the hat on Becca's head. "And you must be careful lest you see the man who chased after you through the woods."

As well as the man who had pursued her into the pasture and the tall man who had stopped by the farm yesterday. Becca's sleep had been fitful, interspersed with dreams of running from two men holding binoculars. She wouldn't worry Hattie, but the sweet Amish woman was right. Becca needed to be watchful not only in town but also here on Hattie's farm.

"I'll be careful, Hattie. You can be assured of that. Zeke is good to take me to town. I appreciate everything both of you have done."

"Soon your memory will return and you can decide whether to go back to the life you knew or to move on and make a new life for yourself. *Gott* will let you know the direction you must take."

"God might answer your prayers, Hattie, but He ignores mine."

The older woman tsked. "Hard though it might be to feel His love during difficult times, we must believe what Scripture tells us."

Becca tugged on the hat. "I'm not sure if Scripture was ever part of my life."

"You are Amish, dear. The Bible is important in your life. You can be sure of this."

Becca couldn't be sure of anything, not when she had no memory. She hesitated for a moment, searching for a Bible verse. None came.

Her stomach growled.

"You are hungry," Hattie stated as if any troublesome situation could be resolved with food.

Becca shook her head. "That's not the problem, Hattie."

The older woman nodded knowingly. "Then it is your concern for what you will learn today. You are anxious. Warm milk will soothe your stomach."

Becca wanted to laugh. Or cry. She wasn't sure which.

"You're making me feel like a young child. Warm milk will not ease my concern, but I appreciate the offer."

She rubbed her hand over her stomach. "Once I am

in town, everything will be better. Fear grows when we anticipate that which is never as bad as we imagine."

"You remember that from your past?"

Becca sighed. "I'm not sure."

Hattie smiled. "No matter who you are, Becca Troyer. You are a smart woman, *yah*?"

She nodded. "I hope I am smart enough to find out who I am."

"And who you were running from, *yah*?" Hattie added.

"Yah." Becca opened the bedroom door and stepped into the hallway. "I will come home from town with information about my past."

At least, that was Becca's hope. Who was she and who had been chasing after her? She needed answers to both questions and she needed those answers now.

Zeke harnessed Sophie to the buggy and led her to the back porch. The kitchen door opened, and an Amish lad stepped outside. Mentally Zeke knew who was wearing the black trousers held up with suspenders, white shirt and overcoat, but even then, he stared for a long moment as if confused by what he saw.

Becca widened her eyes. "The clothing does not work. I can see it in your gaze." She turned to flee back inside.

"Wait." Zeke reached to grab her arm, but she slipped past him.

"Becca," he called again.

She stopped and glanced over her shoulder at him.

"My expression," he quickly continued, "has nothing to do with your clothing, but with my own inability to put what I see together with who I know you to be."

He dropped his hand and paused again before adding, "Hattie was right. You will not be recognized."

Becca smiled weakly. "This is good, *yah?*"

He nodded. *"Yah."*

Not being recognized would be safer for Becca, but seeing her dressed in men's clothing confused Zeke even more. What was wrong with him? Ever since he had spotted her staggering in the middle of the road, his normally calm demeanor had been in turmoil. Was it because she was a woman or was it because she was this particular woman, with green eyes and a hint of coral in her cheeks, who caused him so much unease?

She drew closer and looked up as if somewhat perplexed. "How am I to climb into the buggy?"

Zeke wanted to laugh at her question and the cute way she pouted her mouth as she pondered her problem. Knowing better than to embarrass her, he kept his thoughts to himself and said instead, "You must learn now. When we are in town, I will not be able to help you lest someone wonder why an Amish boy cannot heft himself into the front seat of a buggy."

He pointed to the metal step. "Place one foot here and then swing up onto the seat."

She grabbed the front of the buggy for support, placed her foot where he had indicated and gracefully raised herself onto the seat.

"Gut," he said with a nod once she was settled.

"You will sit next to me?" she asked.

"Yah, but you must remember you are a boy, especially if buggies pass us on the road. Glance down or to the side and keep your hat lowered. Amish children do not speak unless spoken to, which might be difficult for you."

She wrinkled her brow and turned her mouth into a coy grin. "Are you saying I talk a lot?"

"Not at all, but most women enjoy making conversation. A boy would not be as gregarious."

"A boy would be inquisitive and ask questions that would be posed one after the other."

Zeke's lips twitched. "You are forcing me to recall my youth. *Yah*, I had a million questions. It is how a boy learns."

"And I'm sure your father answered each question with patience and understanding."

"My mother answered my questions." He climbed into the buggy and sat next to her.

"And your father?" Becca pressed.

"My *datt* believed children should speak only when called upon to do so, which is something you, as an Amish lad, should remember." Zeke grabbed the reins and encouraged Sophie forward.

"Your dad sounds like a hard taskmaster," Becca said once they were on the main road.

"No more so than other fathers. As you know, the man is the head of the Amish family."

"True, but it sounds as if your *datt* took that role to heart." She hesitated before asking, "Is that why you're living here on the mountain with your aunt?"

"Hattie needs help with her farm," he offered as explanation, in hopes of satisfying her curiosity without having to delve into his own past.

"She could hire help," Becca mused.

"*Yah*, but a family takes care of their own."

"What about your parents, Zeke? Who helps them?"

How could he explain his estrangement with his father without mentioning Irene?

"My *mamm* died a few years ago," he replied, hoping it would suffice.

"And your father?"

"He works his own farm."

Zeke glanced at Becca, wondering how many more questions she would pose. She was as inquisitive as a dozen young lads, only there was nothing boyish about the arch of her brow or the wistful longing he read in her gaze.

She glanced at the passing countryside. "I wish I could remember my parents."

He hated hearing the pain in her voice.

Zeke flicked the reins, needing to think of something other than the woman sitting next to him.

What would Becca think of him if he revealed his own past? Some things were better left unsaid.

Except his memory would not let him forget how he had followed Irene to Petersville only to find her living with a man twice her age, a man who had a meth lab in his cabin and a wad of money in his wallet. A man who had stolen her heart and her common sense just as she had done to Zeke.

He had tried to save her from the burning cabin and had almost gotten killed in his attempt. The explosion played over in his mind, making him shudder.

He turned away from Becca and glanced over his shoulder, hoping she did not see the regret that colored his life. Had he really loved Irene or was he like all young men, running after a pretty girl who made him think not with his head but with his heart?

"Are you all right?" Becca touched his arm, the gesture warm with concern.

He shrugged out of her hold and turned his gaze back to the road. "It is nothing."

She folded her hands on her lap. "You're sure?"

He clenched his jaw and flicked the reins again, speeding the mare along the paved roadway. "I am sure."

The roar of a vehicle sounded behind them. Zeke tightened his hold on the reins just as a van raced around the buggy, going much too fast on the mountain road.

Becca gasped and reached for Zeke's arm as if fearing the passing vehicle's momentum would throw her from the buggy.

The logo on the side of the van read Montcliff Studio. The vehicle accelerated and continued on the road.

The mare balked.

"Easy there, girl. Easy."

Sophie shook her mane and swished her tail, letting Zeke know her upset.

"Was that the man who stopped by the farm yesterday?" Becca asked.

He rubbed her hand, hoping to calm her unease. "I did not see the driver's face. The man in the van who stopped by the farm yesterday is named Larry Landers. He works for the movie studio and wanted to shoot some scenes on Hattie's property."

"I overheard from the kitchen."

"Then you heard him claim the money would be good. He did not understand that some things cannot be bought."

Not love, not happiness, not a father's respect.

He thought of the man who was chasing Becca. What if he was her husband?

Zeke flicked the reins and wondered how things had gotten so convoluted. His status quo, as the *Englisch* would say, was in upheaval. Zeke could feel it in the core of his being. Nothing was in the right order. Not his life. Not his common sense. And not his heart. In fact, his heart more than anything was sending signals he did not understand.

He would not make a mistake about a woman again. Even a pretty woman whose need tugged at his heart.

SIX

Rounding a bend in the road, Zeke's heart pounded a warning. He tugged on the reins, pulling Sophie to a stop.

"Get in the rear of the buggy, Becca."

She glanced at the cars and vans forming a roadblock. A number of men, all wearing jackets bearing the Montcliff Studio logo, had stopped a car heading to town.

"Should we turn around?" she asked.

"Perhaps." But just as Zeke was ready to nudge Sophie into the oncoming lane so they could head back to Hattie's house, a man at the roadblock motioned them forward.

"Pretend you are that young Amish boy."

Zeke knew from Becca's expression that she was worried. So was he.

As soon as she crawled into the rear, he flicked the reins ever so slightly.

"I do not see the man who chased me yesterday morning," Becca said, her voice little more than a whisper.

"That is *gut*. We will trust this is just a minor annoyance and not a problem."

"I hope you're right."

"*Yah*, I hope that, as well."

He pulled in a deep breath to calm himself. Zeke did not want to appear nervous, not when Becca's safety could be in jeopardy.

The car ahead of them had been waved through the roadblock. The vehicle accelerated and headed toward town. If only Zeke's buggy could also be waved through.

A burly man motioned him to a line in the road and then held up his hand, signaling he should halt.

Zeke tugged on the reins. Sophie stopped and shook her head. Perhaps the mare sensed his tension.

The road guard stepped closer. "Where you headed?"

"Is something wrong?" Zeke asked.

The man narrowed his gaze. "Just checking a few cars."

"And the reason for the check?"

The guy shook his head, visibly annoyed. "You Amish struggle with authority."

"I did not know Montcliff Studios controlled the public roadway."

"We've got a multimillion-dollar facility. We want to protect access to our property."

"Something has been stolen?"

The guy peered into the back of the buggy, stared for a long moment at Becca and then nodded to Zeke.

"Have a good day."

Returning the nod, Zeke encouraged the mare forward. Once the buggy had passed through the maze of cars, he encouraged Sophie to pick up the pace.

Becca climbed back into the front seat. "Why did you give him a hard time?"

"I did no such thing."

"You questioned what was going on. I thought he was going to search the buggy."

"And what would he have found?" Zeke asked.

"He would have found me." Her eyes widened as she jammed her thumb against her chest.

"Had I not questioned his right to be stopping vehicles and buggies, he might have been more aggressive."

"I think you're wrong."

"But we got through the roadblock, Becca. Everything went well."

She shifted away from him as if exasperated, or perhaps she was still frightened by the unexpected roadblock. Truth be known, Zeke had been nervous, as well.

Why were the people from the movie studio stopping those who traveled along the roadway? Was it because the movie star had gone missing? Or had someone else disappeared?

He glanced at Becca. Finding a woman in the middle of the road not far from where a missing movie star had worked and then to have people searching the area seemed more than a coincidence. Add the fact that one, if not two, men were running after Becca and the situation became even more convoluted.

Was Becca an Amish woman who had left her family or was she somehow involved with Montcliff Studio? If so, did she know anything about the movie star who had disappeared?

Becca remained silent as Ezekiel encouraged Sophie along the mountain road. She couldn't stop thinking about the roadblock and the two times she had been chased through the woods.

The cool afternoon air tugged at the felt hat she wore. Shivering, she yanked it down on her head, then wrapped the coat across her chest and held it tight at her neck.

Zeke glanced her way. "You are cold?"

"The breeze feels good and the air is fresh and clear."

"No one recognized you, Becca."

She breathed deeply, grateful for Zeke's support.

"Do you have any memory of the movie studio?" he asked.

She shook her head. "What would an Amish woman do there?"

"Perhaps you worked in the kitchen."

"Maybe. I could wash dishes and peel potatoes."

He smiled. "You do not give yourself enough credit. You could run the kitchen."

"I'm glad you have faith in me." She thought for a moment and then added, "Or maybe I live on an Amish farm in the area and have nothing to do with the studio."

"A movie star went missing, Becca, which is probably the reason for the roadblock."

She nodded, mulling over what he had said. Surely she had nothing to do with Montcliff Studio, yet something about the studio logo tugged at her memory.

"How did the studio end up here on Amish Mountain?" she asked.

He shrugged his broad shoulders. "Probably someone vacationed in the area. The *Englisch* rent rooms in town. The Amish community is starting to become a tourist attraction."

"But a movie studio in Georgia seems strange."

"The state gave the motion picture industry a cut on

their taxes. Anything to bring in jobs and grow business."

"Which is not what the Amish want."

"*Yah*, the Amish want their own land and to live without the interference of government. Some people find that difficult to accept."

He turned to face her. "Does this sound strange to you?"

"Why would it? It is the Amish way."

He smiled. Becca could not remember where she came from, but she thought like the Amish. If only she would learn more about her past.

"People gawk as they drive by the farm," Zeke continued to explain. "Perhaps they have never seen the Amish. I heard the studio needed mountainous terrain for a film. They shot a short documentary here first and then entered into a contract to rent the land."

"No doubt, from an *Englischer*," Becca added.

"An *Englischer* who had been Amish. Levi Gingerich left the Amish way and took his children with him, as well. He owns a sizable portion of land on the mountain, just as my father does."

"Yet your father doesn't live here."

"He lives closer to town and is now the bishop of the local district. He owns Hattie's farm and more acreage that is currently unsettled."

"Will your father pass the land on to you someday?"

Zeke shrugged. "I have a brother who would be his first choice."

"Older or younger?"

"Older, but he and his wife moved away from the area."

"Does the youngest son usually take care of the parents?" she asked.

"That sometimes happens, but my father does not want my help."

Something Becca doubted, but she remained silent and turned to study the scenery.

Dense forests of thick pine trees covered the land on each side of the road interspersed with barren hardwoods that had lost their leaves. Some still lay scattered on the ground, holding a portion of their fall colors.

The memory of running through the woods returned with a jolt. She wrapped her arms across her chest, recalling the footfalls of not only the man chasing her in the night but also the man who had come after her the next morning.

"Your memory will return," Zeke stated, as if he understood her struggle.

A farmhouse appeared in the distance. "This is the Troyer land, Becca. We will stop here before going to Willkommen."

She swallowed down the concern that filled her. "What if they recognize me?"

"They will see an Amish youth. Not an Amish woman. I will ask if they know of anyone missing in their family while you remain in the buggy."

Becca straightened her shoulders and peered into the distance.

"Slouch down," Zeke said.

"What?"

"Put your elbows on your knees and lean forward as a boy would do."

She followed his prompting, but kept her eyes focused on the farmhouse. Three young boys stood on the porch. Two older boys stepped from the barn as the buggy came to a stop.

Zeke hopped to the ground and turned as a man called to him from the nearby paddock.

"Is it Ezekiel Hochstetler?" the man asked jovially in greeting. *"Wie gehtes?"*

"*Gut*, Willie," Zeke responded. "And how is the family?"

"The children grow like weeds. Ida has coffee if you care for a cup."

"Not today but thank you."

"What brings you down the mountain?"

"I am going to town for supplies. We heard talk that a woman named Troyer had gone missing. Hattie wanted me to check to see if she could be your kin?"

Willie Troyer was medium height and stocky in build. He wiped a thick hand over his square jaw and peered into the distance for a long moment as if thinking if anyone had gone missing. "This I have not heard. Surely, we would know of anyone in the family. Was the woman in need?"

Zeke shrugged. "I know nothing more. News travels. Sometimes it changes as it goes."

"Like the game the children play," Willie said with a nod. "They whisper a statement from child to child that ends up different at the end. It is the same as we grow older. Only what starts as news, ends as gossip."

"I will tell Hattie that your family is well."

"Have you seen your father, Zeke?"

"He is busy."

"The years pass. Do not let them slip away before it is too late."

"He knows where to find me, Willie, yet I appreciate your concern."

Zeke turned back to the buggy.

"Who's the boy?" the farmer asked.

Becca's heart lurched. She glanced at the children as if she had not heard the question.

"A boy from the mountain. He helps Hattie at times."

"Did a man from the studio talk to you about renting land on which to film?"

"Larry Landers stopped by yesterday. Hattie rejected his offer."

Willie nodded. "Hattie made a wise decision. I told him my farm was not to be used for *Englischer* movies. He did not like my answer."

"He does not understand the Amish way."

"That is for certain. The bishop should talk to the studio manager so they understand us better."

"You tell the bishop what he needs to do, Willie. He will listen to you."

"He will listen to his son if you speak to him, Zeke."

Shaking his head, Zeke moved closer to the buggy. "Good to see you, Willie."

"Good to have you back on Amish Mountain, Ezekiel. A man is not held responsible for what he does in his youth before baptism, *yah*?"

"Perhaps you think that way. Some do not. Leaving the community was a grievous wrong as far as my *datt* was concerned."

"Time has passed. Things change."

"The seasons change, but my father's heart remains the same."

"Take care of yourself, Zeke."

"You, as well."

He climbed into the buggy and turned the mare back to the road. Becca remained silent as if she were truly that Amish boy, who lived on the mountain.

From what Ezekiel had said, the disagreement with his father was more than a family squabble. At least Zeke knew who he was and what had happened in his past.

Was Becca caught in the middle of a family squabble? She didn't belong to the Troyers who lived at the foot of Amish Mountain. Was there another family to whom she was related? Had someone from that Troyer family chased after her? Could that be the same man who had come after her today or were they two different people? She cringed thinking of terrible scenarios that could be part of her forgotten life.

After leaving the Troyer farm, Zeke guided the mare onto the main road, heading to Willkommen. The town would be bustling today and hopefully something or someone would trigger Becca's memory. He needed to be careful. Keeping Becca safe was his top priority.

"Evidently Troyer is not my last name," she said with a sigh.

"Troyer is a common Amish name. You are not part of that Troyer family, but there are others. The sheriff may know of a missing person report."

"I… I do not want to involve the authorities."

He glanced at her, seeing the concern that troubled her gaze. Was she wary of law enforcement because of her past? Or was she just being cautious?

"It is an option, Becca, and perhaps the fastest way to get information. I will be discreet."

"But you will not tell a lie."

"You know this about me?" he asked, surprised that she would make such a statement.

"You are a *gut* man, Ezekiel. I have seen how attentive you are to Hattie. I do not wish you to do anything against your will because of me."

"I would never lie, but all details do not need to be revealed, *yah*?"

She smiled and nodded. "You're right."

"You do not need to worry, Becca."

"I'm not worried."

"Ah, but now *you* stretch the truth. I see it in your eyes. You fear what you might learn today."

"Suppose I am married to a hateful man? Suppose he tried to hurt me? Suppose…suppose I have children."

"Would you leave children behind to save yourself?"

"Never."

"See, you have answered the question for yourself. You were running away from something, and yes, it could be from a husband. But you did not leave children behind. I am certain of this."

Becca's faint sigh of relief warmed his heart and made him see the folly of his own thoughts that she could be involved in something suspect. She was not the woman from his past. Irene had never been content on the mountain or with her own life. She always wanted more and was fascinated with the allure of the world. He had been young and fickle back then, not realizing the qualities he desired in a woman.

And Becca? his inner voice questioned.

Was she a desirable woman?

He flicked the reins, not yet ready to answer such a query. Not until he knew more about the real Becca Troyer.

SEVEN

Becca's heart pounded with apprehension as they drove into town. Shops lined the streets and people milled about on the sidewalks. Buggies were everywhere, along with Amish women in long dresses and white bonnets, ushering their children across the pedestrian walkways at various intersections. Bearded men wearing wide-brimmed hats guided their horses along the busy thoroughfares and turned into vacant lots at the rear of the businesses where the horses would be tethered while the families shopped.

"So many people are in town today," Becca said breathlessly, trying to take in all the activity around her.

"There is a cattle auction. Many of the farmers come to town and bring their families. They shop and then bid on cattle so the trip serves more than one purpose."

"The children are not in school?"

"Today there is no school because of the auction."

She glanced right and then left, all the while studying faces, the young, the old, men, women, Amish, *Englisch*.

"Drive more slowly, Zeke. I want to see everything." There were so many people, and she feared missing the one person who would open up the past to her.

Zeke tugged back ever so lightly on the reins. The mare responded. "The cattle auction is on one of the side streets. We will drive there first." Zeke guided Sophie onto a more narrow road and then into the expansive complex that included an open-air pavilion and a large building with a sign over the door that read Cattle Auction.

Horses were tethered to hitching posts in front and rows of buggies lined the grassy knoll to the rear of the complex. A horse barn sat nearby.

Men chatted amicably in the central asphalt area. Young boys stood near their fathers and matched their own stances to the older men's. Women grouped together with the young children, and girls chatted nearby.

"Is there a flea market today?" Becca asked, reading the sign on the pavilion that mentioned the market.

"It is held once a month on the first Wednesday. We can come back then. I thought today might provide an opportunity to search for your family."

If only the search would be productive.

"See anything that looks familiar?" he asked.

She shook her head and tried to shrug off the discouragement that weighed her down as if a hundred-pound sack of potatoes rested on her shoulders.

"There is more to explore," Zeke assured her as he guided the mare toward the auction exit that returned them to the street.

Drivers in passing buggies waved, and Zeke nodded in response. Becca was careful to lower her eyes whenever anyone stared at her too intently. Thankfully most of the people were not interested in a young boy.

"The sheriff's office is on the next block," Zeke said.

"I do not want to stop there."

"We will pass by."

Her stomach churned. In the distance, she saw the sign for the sheriff's department. A number of men stood on the sidewalk, all with broad shoulders and thick necks. Could one of them have been the man chasing her? Was he there now, telling the sheriff about his missing wife or daughter or sister?

Glancing down a side road, Becca's chest tightened. She tapped Ezekiel's hand. "Look to your right. Is that the same van that passed us on the road earlier?"

Zeke peered at the vehicle. "Perhaps. Although the studio seems to have a number of vans. No telling who drove that particular vehicle to town."

Returning her gaze to the sheriff's office, she spied the tall, muscular man from yesterday, wearing a jacket that bore the Montcliff Studio logo.

She nudged Zeke.

"Yah," he said. "That is Larry Landers, who stopped by Hattie's farm."

"And the Troyer place."

Zeke nodded. "I do not think he will find any Amish farmers agreeing to give him access to their land."

Landers stared at Zeke and then flicked his gaze to Becca as the buggy passed the sheriff's office. Her mouth went dry, and a roar filled her ears. Something about his expression unsettled her.

She glanced away, trying to mimic a disinterested youth. Heat burned her cheeks, and she hoped her flushed face would not bring more scrutiny either to herself or to Ezekiel.

Grateful when Zeke turned at the next intersection, she glanced back. The man was still staring at the buggy.

Was there a connection between her and Larry Landers? Troubled as she was, Becca refused to share her concern with Zeke. If she did not understand her own feelings, he would not, as well.

Besides, she was probably overreacting. The man had startled her as he drove down the mountain, going much too fast. Surely that was the reason for her unrest. That and nothing else.

Then she thought of him watching Hattie's house with binoculars. The sweet Amish woman had told Becca to be careful, which meant she needed to keep her eyes on Landers. She didn't want to be taken by surprise and forced to flee for her life again.

Zeke guided the buggy through a number of side streets, hoping to trigger Becca's memory. "Do you see anything that brings back memories?"

She shook her head and sighed. "Nothing that I can recognize. What if this trip to town provides no clues to my past and turns out to be a waste of time?"

"Do not get discouraged, Becca. There is more to see. Besides, one clue could open up your past. We will not give up this soon."

At the next intersection, Zeke spied Larry Landers climbing from a studio van now parked farther down the street. He hurried into an office building. "Mr. Landers must have business in town."

"He seems to be everywhere, which worries me, Zeke."

"Do not let him concern you, Becca. He is probably still looking for that perfect location for the filming."

"We spoke of it earlier, but it does seem strange to have a movie studio in an Amish community," Becca said.

"What was once unheard of becomes the norm. It is the way of the *Englisch* world. We Amish keep our lives the same and trace our traditions back hundreds of years. There is something good about that consistency."

"It sounds as if you do not welcome change."

He thought of the new woman who had stumbled into his life.

Before he had a chance to answer, Becca added, "Sometimes things change without us wanting them to do so."

He understood her upset. "Your memory will return, Becca."

He leaned closer. "Glance down the street. Do you see anything familiar? Or do you recognize anyone?"

Slowly she studied the shops and the people who walked along the street and then turned back to Zeke. "I recognize no one except you."

She glanced again at the studio van parked by the curb. "But something about the logo on the van tugs at my memory."

"You saw Landers at Hattie's house. He is a man one does not forget, especially as he asserts what he thinks is his authority."

Zeke encouraged Sophie through an intersection. "Remember too that Landers has been stopping at farms in the area. Perhaps he stopped at the farm where you lived. You could have seen him there."

"If that is true, it means my home is not far from here." She scrunched down lower in the seat. "If so, someone might recognize me."

Seeing the concern on her face, he dropped his voice, hoping to reassure her once again. "You are dressed in men's clothing. No one will make the connection."

She nodded and started to say something, then stopped as they passed two men on the sidewalk. They both wore the Montcliff Studio logo on their jackets.

"Caleb mentioned the studio was filming in town," Zeke said. "Perhaps that is the reason so many movie people are here today."

Becca glanced at the men. "I don't recognize either of them."

"Does the logo on their jackets bring back memories?"

"Not like the van parked on the street. Perhaps it is the van and not the logo."

"Perhaps."

"Could we drive around the countryside before returning to Hattie's farm?" she asked. "If Larry Landers did stop at my home, then I must live close to Amish Mountain."

"This we can do after we have seen everything in town."

He turned onto another street and pulled up on the reins, bringing Sophie to a stop. The entire block was cordoned off by a wooden fence, more than fifteen feet tall, that prevented anyone from seeing into the enclosed area.

Signs tacked to the fencing read Montcliff Studio. Filming in Progress. A number of men dressed in navy blue uniforms patrolled the outside of the giant barricade. Montcliff Security was stamped on their jackets.

"Montcliff Studio likes privacy," Becca said. "They put up fencing so no one can see what's going on at the filming."

Zeke nodded. "This is a first for Willkommen."

He spied one of the deputies that worked for the sheriff's department standing farther down the street. Zeke had known Mike Frazier in his youth.

"There is a hitching post behind the leather goods store," Zeke told Becca. "I will leave you there with the buggy while I talk to Deputy Frazier. He has only recently started working for the sheriff's department."

Becca grabbed his hand. "I told you I do not want to involve law enforcement."

"I will not reveal anything about you, Becca, but I need to let someone at the sheriff's office know about the roadblock. This is not something we want to face again. I also will ask about any missing person reports."

"And what if the deputy suspects I'm the person who's missing?"

"Trust me, Becca. Mike Frazier is a *gut* man."

The expression on her face told him she had a hard time trusting anyone. Truth be told, he could understand her concern about involving law enforcement. With no memory about her past and knowing she had been running away, Becca had to be careful.

Zeke guided the mare to the rear of the building where a number of other rigs were parked. He climbed down from the buggy and tied the reins to the post. "Stay here, Becca. I will be back shortly."

He hurried to the main street and waved a greeting. "*Gut* to see you, Mike. I heard you were working for the sheriff." Zeke smiled as he approached his friend.

"News travels even to Amish Mountain. What brings you to town, Zeke?"

"My aunt had some need of provisions, and I wanted to check out the cattle auction later today."

"I hear Hattie's farm is making a turnaround with your management."

Zeke shrugged off the compliment. "A woman of years living alone cannot do the work of a younger man. I am happy to help, and she provides a room and food that will make me fat if I do not curb my appetite."

Mike chuckled. "My father always said Hattie was the best cook in the area."

"How is your father?"

"Getting more and more infirmed. He's living at the assisted living center in town. With me working various shifts, there was no one at home to take care of him. His balance is not good and his mind is starting to wander. I worried about his safety in the hours that I was away from the house."

"It is hard to know what to do, *yah*?"

"I saw your dad last week when I took my father to the doctor."

Zeke's heart hitched. "My *datt* needed medical care?"

"Even the Amish get sick, Zeke."

"Yet my father has not been one to visit *Englisch* doctors."

"One gets older and wiser with years. He said it was a routine visit."

Even the mention of a routine visit did not ease Zeke's concern about his father's well-being. They had been estranged for two years, but the father-son bond would remain forever, even if his father was not interested in having a relationship with his wayward son.

"Montcliff Studio is a big attraction today," Zeke said, pointing to the giant fences.

"They're filming in town all this week, which means more traffic. Everyone wants to see a movie star.

Thankfully, they've got their own security folks, but the sheriff's department is working overtime to make sure everything runs smoothly."

"Any problems?"

Mike shook his head. "Everything has been peaceful and that makes me happy."

Zeke thought of the woman who had disrupted his own peace. He had to be careful about what he said to the deputy. Zeke needed information, but he did not want to cause Becca harm.

"I stopped at Troyer's farm on my way to town today," Zeke said. "Hattie heard one of Willie's relatives was missing, but Willie Troyer said it was no one he knew. You have perhaps learned something about a missing person?"

Mike rubbed his chin. "No word on any Troyers. A man from Montcliff Studio stopped in and mentioned the star of the film they're working on left the area for a bit. He seemed concerned but didn't want to file a missing person report."

Zeke stepped closer. "Why would he tell you this?"

The deputy shrugged. "He acted as if he wanted information."

Which was what Zeke wanted, as well. "Did he tell you the name of the missing movie star?"

"Vanessa Harrington. He showed me her picture. She's a looker. Evidently married, but she's been separated from her husband for the last few months. The studio thinks she returned home, yet she's not answering her cell phone. The studio producer flew to California in hopes of bringing her back here to complete the film."

"Sounds like she thinks only of herself and not the

other people working on the film. Has anyone else gone missing?"

The deputy looked quizzically at Zeke. "One missing movie star is enough."

Zeke smiled as if making light of his comment. "I wondered because of the roadblock the studio people put up on Amish Mountain."

"What are you talking about?"

"Men wearing Montcliff Studio jackets blocked the road with their vehicles. They stopped my buggy and glanced inside."

"Did they tell you why?"

"I thought it was because of that missing movie star."

The deputy let out a deep breath. "I'll pass the information on to the sheriff. Someone needs to inform the studio that the road is maintained by the county and patrolled by the sheriff's office. They have no right to set up any type of roadblock."

The deputy shook his head. "Thanks for letting me know, Zeke. By the way, Caleb Gingerich got a job at the studio."

"Have you seen him recently?" Zeke asked.

Mike smiled. "He showed me his new convertible. That guy lives above his paycheck, just like his dad. His sister had problems too, wanting what she didn't have and couldn't afford."

Zeke gut tightened.

Mike's eyes widened. "Look, I'm sorry, Zeke. I wasn't thinking. You and Irene were an item, as I recall. Didn't you follow her to Petersville? Terrible about the explosion and fire. Meth's a killer in more ways than one."

Zeke knew that all too well.

"If my memory serves me right, you had a run-in with the law," the deputy continued. "Didn't they suspect you were responsible for her death?"

"I was found innocent and released, Mike. That was a long time ago."

"A couple years, right?" He slapped Zeke's shoulder. "I'm really sorry I brought it up."

Zeke was sorry too, sorry he had talked to Mike and mentioned a missing woman. Becca had cautioned him not to get involved with law enforcement. He should have heeded her warning.

EIGHT

Becca had scooted to the front of the buggy where she watched Zeke as he talked to the deputy sheriff. No matter what he said about not revealing her identity to law enforcement, she was concerned that he might say something inadvertently.

Feeling somewhat conspicuous staring at them from the front seat, she had crawled down on the far side of the buggy and stood next to Sophie. Rubbing the mare's mane, she peered at the two men, feeling much less obvious.

She noticed the studio van parked farther down the street. Her stomach tightened as Larry Landers stepped out of one of the buildings. He hurried toward his van, then glanced at where she stood.

More than anything, she wanted to crawl into the back of the buggy and hide, but before she could do so, he started walking along the sidewalk, heading in her direction.

She looked over her shoulder and spied a narrow alleyway with a Dempsey dumpster that would provide the perfect cover if he drew near and passed by on the sidewalk.

When he stopped at the intersection, waiting for the light to change, Becca scurried into the alley and hunkered down behind the dumpster. From that hiding spot, she lost sight of Zeke. She didn't want him to return to the buggy and then wonder where she had gone. She especially didn't want Zeke to act upset about not finding her when Larry Landers was nearby.

Hearing the footfalls of an approaching pedestrian, she peered over the top of the dumpster, then ducked as Landers came into view. He stopped for a long moment before stepping into the alley.

Becca trembled, expecting to be found out.

A car horn sounded. Landers hurried back to the corner as if to see what had happened.

Wanting to evade discovery, Becca ran along the alleyway and turned onto the next street. She stepped toward a nearby store and stopped to catch her breath. Although worried Zeke would return to the buggy and discover she wasn't there, she was even more worried about Landers.

She watched the street for a few minutes. A studio van turned at a distant intersection, heading in the opposite direction from where she was standing. Evidently Landers had left the area. Relieved, she retraced her steps, needing to return to the buggy.

As she hurried around the corner, she stopped short and almost collided with the tall man from the movie studio.

"Why are you running away from me?" Landers lunged for her.

She ran back to the main street, past the store where she had caught her breath and turned onto another side street.

Glancing over her shoulder, she saw him racing after her. Her head felt like it would explode, and her mouth went dry as his footsteps grew louder.

She slowed at an intersection snarled with traffic.

He caught up to her and grabbed her arm. She gasped, jerked free and ran into the street, directly in front of an oncoming vehicle. The driver braked to a stop, then laid on the horn and raised his fist.

Ignoring his show of anger, she dashed around the car and raced to the opposite curb.

A gust of wind tugged at her hat, lifting it from her head. She caught it in time, but not before her long hair spilled around her shoulders.

She looked back.

Surprise washed over Landers's angular face.

"Stop!" he called from the far corner, still stalled by the traffic.

The light changed, and he crossed the street. "Wait up!"

She turned down another alleyway. The path forked left. She took it, her feet pounding the pavement.

Her chest burned, and she gasped for air, but she pushed forward, needing to distance herself from the *Englischer*. If he caught her, he might haul her off to the very place from which she had tried to escape.

She pulled in another deep breath and counted the cadence of her feet slapping the pavement to keep her mind off the danger following much too closely.

The main road through town appeared in the distance. She glanced right, then left. Where could she hide?

Her hair hung free. She shoved it into her hat and yanked the wide brim down on her forehead.

A farm truck turned left at the corner, hauling a steer in a wire pen.

The auction. She raced around the corner, relieved to see the outdoor pavilion and a crowd of people who would provide the cover she needed.

After leaving the deputy, Zeke returned to where he had parked the buggy, expecting to find Becca hiding in the rear. When he peered inside, his gut tightened. The buggy was empty and Becca was gone.

His stomach tightened, and a warning rang in his ears.

Zeke clutched his fists, anger and fear bubbling up within him, anger at himself for not keeping better watch over Becca and fear for her safety.

He hurried to the corner and glanced in both directions, searching for some sign of an Amish lad. A number of women chatted amicably in the distance. Two young girls in black bonnets and long dresses stood near their mothers. He was looking for a slender Amish boy with expressive eyes and a fearful gaze.

Where was she? Why had Becca gone missing again?

Becca slipped through the throng of people milling around outside the cattle auction, hoping to elude Larry Landers. A number of Amish families stood together near the Flea Market Pavilion. The children, a mix of boys and girls, chatted nearby.

Sidling closer to the group, she stopped long enough to glance back. Landers stood at the entrance to the parking area, hands on his hips, and studied the crowd. Not wanting to draw his attention, she stepped even

closer to the Amish youth and hoped no one would ask
who she was and why she was standing so near to them.

All the while, she kept her gaze on Landers. Tall
as he was, the location manager was easy to spot. He
walked around the periphery of the market and kept
staring into the fray. Thankfully, he didn't pick her out
of the crowd. After what seemed like an eternity, he
shrugged and walked out of the market area. Becca
watched as he headed back to the street and turned
north, retracing his steps.

Relieved he was gone, she moved away from the
other youths and breathed out a lungful of pent-up air.
Although grateful for the Amish gathering, she needed
to find Ezekiel. After all this time, he had probably
finished his conversation with the deputy and had realized she was missing. As generous as he and Hattie
had been, she didn't want to cause him more concern.

Needing to return to where he had parked the buggy,
she started toward the exit and passed through a thick
crowd of Amish folks heading toward the auction house.
A few of the people offered a greeting, which warmed
her heart. Instead of being recognized, the Amish community was embracing her. Becca smiled at the thought
and let down her guard.

Someone grabbed her arm. "What are you doing
here?"

Her heart stopped as she looked into the Amish
man's eyes. He was tall and muscular, with a full beard
and a clean-shaven upper lip. His shoulder-length hair
was topped with a black felt hat. As authentically Amish
as he appeared, something about his expression seemed
artificial.

Peering more closely, she realized his face was covered with a heavy layer of pancake makeup. Dark pencil colored his brows and lined his eyes. The man wasn't Amish, he was acting the part.

"You're coming with me," he snarled.

She shoved him with her free hand. "Get away from me."

He tightened his grip on her arm.

A group of real Amish men stood nearby. "Help me," she called, trying to jerk free of his hold. "He's hurting me."

Oblivious to her plight, the men smiled and nodded among themselves.

Raising her foot, she kicked the guy's shin.

His eyes widened.

She kicked him again and again. "Help!"

He groaned. His grip eased ever so slightly.

She jerked free of his hold and ran into the crowd.

The actor followed after her, favoring his good leg.

She dashed toward the stable, hearing the man's footfalls behind her. The cloying scent of straw and horse surrounded her as she ducked into the dark interior. An Amish boy, probably thirteen or fourteen years old, was mucking one of the stalls.

He stopped and leaned on his rake. "Is something wrong?"

"A man's following me. I need to get away from him."

Glancing through the open doorway, she saw the actor drawing closer to the stable.

"How can I get to the main road?"

The kid pointed to an exit in the rear. "Turn right at the dirt road. It will take you there."

"Danki." She raced out of the stable.

Looking back, she saw the man trip and fall. The kid apologized for his rake getting in the way.

"An accident," the stable boy insisted, all the while the actor raised his voice and shook his fist at the boy.

His raucousness attracted a number of other Amish men who streamed into the stable, no doubt, to determine what was amiss. Becca would have chuckled if she hadn't been so unnerved by what had happened.

Everyone seemed to be after her. A man in a black car with a man bun, Larry Landers and now an actor dressed like an Amish man. Her heart sank as she followed the dirt path that headed toward the main road. If only she could jar her memory. What had she done to cause so many people to chase after her?

NINE

Ezekiel searched on foot throughout the downtown area, but he found no trace of Becca. His heart ached, fearing something terrible had happened.

Two years ago, he had lost Irene.

Now he had lost Becca.

Overcome with worry, he returned to his buggy and climbed into the seat he had shared with her earlier. He grabbed the reins and encouraged Sophie forward. As the mare trotted along the main road, Zeke studied the various businesses and shops and then peered down each of the side streets, hoping he could find her.

He started to turn the mare around so they could head back to where the studio was filming and search again.

Movement in an alleyway caught his eye. He eased back on the reins and stared at the spot, unable to determine what he had seen.

A swatch of chestnut hair? Or was it only his imagination?

He tethered Sophie to a hitching post and ran along the sidewalk.

Approaching the alley, he saw nothing and derided

himself for his foolishness. Discouraged, he turned back to the buggy.

"Zeke?"

Glancing over his shoulder, he saw Becca peering at him from behind a doorway. Eyes wide, face drawn, she looked scared and frail and confused.

He ran to her and took her into his arms.

"Oh, Becca, I feared losing you." The words tumbled out, one after the other. "I searched but could not find you. Are you all right?"

"Larry Landers followed me to the cattle auction." She clutched his arms and stared into his eyes. "I disappeared into the crowd, and he finally gave up looking for me. I—I planned to find you when an actor dressed like an Amish man grabbed my arm. He wanted me to go with him."

"Did he hurt you?"

"No, because I ran away, just as I did before, but he was a hateful man who raised his voice and shouted at a young stable hand who helped me escape."

"Mike Frazier needs to know."

"The sheriff's deputy?" She shook her head. "Suppose I did something wrong, Zeke. Law enforcement might be looking for me, as well."

Zeke wanted to reassure Becca, but he knew her fears could be real. Much as he did not want to believe anything bad about her, people were searching for Becca. If only he knew why.

Becca shivered in Zeke's arms and wanted to stay wrapped in the warmth of his embrace. Instead he pointed her toward the buggy.

"We must hurry. It is not safe for you to be in town."

He was right, of course.

Stepping out of his arms, she sighed at the sudden letdown she felt.

"I… I'm so glad you found me, Zeke. I thought the main road led to the mountain, but I wasn't sure if you had already passed by here."

He put his hand on the small of her back and guided her forward. All the while, he glanced around them, no doubt to ensure they were not being followed.

Upon reaching the buggy, he helped her into the seat and climbed in next to her. With the flick of the reins, the mare started to trot, the buggy swaying in a steady side-to-side rhythm. Becca slid closer once they left town.

The air was cold, and he wrapped his arm around her as if realizing she needed his warmth and comfort after all that had happened.

Grateful that Zeke had rescued her once again, she eagerly shared how the man had chased after her.

"You are sure he was not the man who came after you in the woods?" Zeke asked.

She shrugged. "I am not sure. The man that night was shouting, and I couldn't make out what he said. Plus, I never saw his face."

Zeke turned to gaze into her eyes.

The concern she saw touched her to the core.

"The memory of running through the woods haunts me, Ezekiel, and comes in my dreams to wake me in the night."

"Yet the actor today knows you."

"Unless he mistook me for someone else. We need to find out if the studio employs any Amish," she stated. "Maybe I did have a job there."

"Caleb Gingerich works in the studio's dining facility."

"The commissary?" she asked.

Zeke raised his brow.

"It's what the dining area is called," she explained.

"You know this how?"

She shook her head. "Perhaps because I did work there."

"The Gingerich house is on the way to Hattie's farm. We will stop there. Caleb may be at home."

"Can we trust him?"

Zeke thought for a moment and then smiled. "Caleb is more interested in his shiny new car than he is in anything else. Plus, I do not think he knows much about the movie business. He will not be a problem."

The word *problem* kept running through Becca's mind as they rode in silence up the mountain. She was a problem. A problem to Hattie and to Zeke, a problem without a past and no hope for the future until she knew more about who she was and what she had been running from two nights ago.

She glanced at Zeke, seeing the determination on his face. As much as she appreciated his help, she also worried about how he would feel once he learned the truth about her past. Suppose she was married or committed to marry someone else? Someone she did not know well enough or did not truly love.

Zeke was a good man. He had helped her so much. Could she be drawn to one man, all the while forgetting about another man from her past?

She tried to shake off the fear of the unknown that was like a ball of fire in her stomach. Shrugging out of Zeke's hold, she scooted to the side of the buggy.

"Are you all right?" he asked.

"A bit woozy."

"You are sick?"

How could she tell him the sickness she was feeling was a sickness of heart, thinking of all that might eventually be revealed?

Tears burned her eyes. She didn't want to know the truth. She wanted to return to Hattie's farm and be surrounded by the older woman's warmth as she and Zeke got to know each other better. The future could be filled with wonderful expectation, if it weren't for the fact that she knew nothing about her former life.

She touched the knot on her head, wishing she would remember more about that night.

"You feel sick because of the bump on your head, Becca. It has not been that long. Rest on my shoulder."

But she didn't want to move closer to Zeke. She was already too close and too drawn to him.

She couldn't allow her heart free rein, like he was giving to the mare, when she had a whole history she needed to uncover.

She closed her eyes and rubbed her hand over her stomach, hoping to ease the unrest she felt.

Zeke was right in taking her to his friend's house. She couldn't live in this twilight world not knowing who she was and what had happened to her. She needed information, and the only way to learn about her past was to confront it head-on, no matter what she uncovered, and no matter who she had been or what had happened to her.

TEN

Zeke was growing more confused by the hour. Having Becca in his arms earlier had sent his emotions into a wild spiral so that he felt out of control and unsure of who he was or what was right about his life. Becca's expression proved she was equally confused.

Larry Landers and an actor had chased after her today. Two men running after Becca only doubled the problem. Add the man at Hattie's house and man who had chased her the first night and the number rose to four.

After Irene's death, he had promised himself to live a quiet life, working hard on Hattie's farm and staying away from anything that might pull him astray.

Yet here he was again, drawn to another woman, a woman who made his heart race and his chest constrict whenever she drew close. Like now.

Becca had snuggled next to him when they had first climbed into the buggy. Her nearness had made his heart warm. Then something had happened—was it something he had said?—and she had slipped away from him.

His father had warned him of fickle women who would steal his heart and leave him in the lurch, so tied up in knots that he would do anything to be with them. Case in point, Irene. He had been smitten by her charms, but he was young then and unknowing in the ways of love and the world.

He focused on the road ahead, needing to calm his upset and focus on finding information about Becca. He had to be firm and not let himself be drawn into another woman's drama, especially a woman who was clueless about her past. Or was Becca pretending to know nothing about the men who had chased after her?

He wanted to believe her, but he had been burned before. He would not play with fire again.

Going to the Gingerich farm was probably another mistake. He had made too many. Irene's father had accused him of causing his daughter's death. Losing a child was the greatest tragedy a person would ever have to endure, and if Levi Gingerich wanted to believe Zeke had caused Irene's death, he would allow the older man to wallow in the untruth. What good would it do to reveal that his daughter had died in a meth lab explosion, and that Zeke had carried her from the cabin and tried to save her life?

Zeke would not repeat the memory that was so painful and so tragic. Nor would her father accept what Zeke said. He was intent on blaming Zeke for his daughter's mistakes.

Levi Gingerich did not need to know the truth. And Zeke did not need to cause anyone more pain. Not Irene's father, not Caleb or his own father…and certainly not Becca.

When all this was over, Zeke would leave the area and find a new Amish community. Surely, someone would need an extra farmhand to help with the livestock and crops. He could trade his work for room and board. *Gott* would provide. At least, he hoped He would.

Zeke guided the mare onto a narrow dirt path that led from the main paved roadway.

"Hold on," he cautioned as they jostled back and forth.

Becca grabbed the side of the seat and then scooted away from the edge, as if fearing she would fall from the buggy.

"Levi needs to fill in the ruts," he told her. "The farm might be in as much disrepair as the access road."

Zeke's hunch was right. Rounding the next bend, he spied the Gingerich farm in the distant twilight. The house, a two-story, white sideboard with a front and back porch, listed as if pulled by the wind and gave evidence of needing refurbishment and repair. The fence posts had rotted and some appeared ready to topple over so that Zeke wondered how the livestock were contained, although when he searched the hillside, he saw only a few head of cattle. The fields looked barren and not because of a fall harvest. They appeared to have lain fallow for more than one planting season.

Uneasy about what he saw, Zeke turned the mare onto the path leading to the house and pulled to a stop near the back porch.

"Stay in the buggy," he told Becca under his breath.

Her eyes were wide as she took in the run-down farmhouse.

A few chickens pecked at the ground, searching for some morsel to eat, a bug or worm or piece of grain. Glancing at the barn, he spied the chicken coop with torn wire that would allow a hungry fox or coyote to take the chickens and their eggs.

Zeke had not seen Mr. Gingerich since the day he had returned to Amish Mountain. He had come here that afternoon to offer his condolences to Irene's grieving father. Only, he had been run off with a shotgun and Levi Gingerich's anger and the warning that he would shoot Zeke the next time he stepped foot on his land.

Hopefully, the old man had mellowed with time.

As Zeke hopped down from the buggy, the door of the house opened and the barrel of a rifle poked through the opening.

Mr. Gingerich stood in the threshold of the door. His eyes narrowed, and a sneer tugged at his thin lips.

"Get outta here, you varmint. Did you forget what I told you the last time I saw you?"

Zeke took a step forward. "No, sir. I remember, but I need to talk to your son."

"You killed my daughter. Now you plan to harm Caleb? Stay away from him so he doesn't wind up dead like Irene."

"Mr. Gingerich, I need to talk to Caleb about the movie studio where he works."

"You Amish don't want me to rent my land. You're trying to undermine my business agreement with the studio, just like your bishop dad."

Zeke's gut tightened. "You talked to my *datt*?"

The older man nodded. "He does not want the movie people in the area. None of the Amish are happy about the venture. They usually keep to themselves, but this time, the Amish are taking a stand."

He stepped onto the porch, the rifle still raised and aimed at Zeke. "Tell your father that I will not change the contract. The studio will stay whether he and his church district like it or not."

Zeke held up a hand. "That's not the reason I'm here."

The old man's eyes widened. "Then state your business before I decide to fill you with lead."

"It has to do with whether Montcliff Studio hires the Amish. Did Caleb mention seeing Amish employees at the studio?"

"Why would the Amish have anything to do with the movie industry?"

"That is what I am trying to determine, Mr. Gingerich."

"He's working tonight, but I doubt he'll talk to you. He knows the way I feel."

"Some things are not as they seem," Zeke insisted.

The man shook his head. "You're responsible for my daughter's death. I will never forgive you."

He glanced at the buggy and spied Becca, still dressed like an Amish lad. "Children are not safe in your presence. I thought I spread the word through the community that you are not to be trusted." He headed for the buggy.

"Come here, lad. You should not be with this man." Gingerich's beady eyes narrowed even more. "He might hurt you."

"Ezekiel Hochstetler is a *gut* man," Becca said from the buggy. "I am sorry about your daughter, but do not blame Zeke for something that was not his doing."

Levi narrowed his gaze. "Why would a young boy speak this way to an old man?"

"I mean you no disrespect, sir."

"We did not mean to upset you, Mr. Gingerich." Zeke climbed onto the buggy, grabbed the reins and encouraged Sophie forward. The old man was becoming deranged and even more militant, but he was right. Zeke should not have come to his farm, and he never should have brought Becca.

She gazed straight ahead, eyes wide, lips drawn. What was she thinking?

Probably that Zeke was as confused and misguided as Levi Gingerich.

Becca remained silent all the while Zeke encouraged Sophie along the bumpy access path and then onto the main roadway.

"Mr. Gingerich doesn't seem to like you," Becca finally said.

"An understatement for sure. He believes I was involved in his daughter's death."

"Why didn't you tell him the truth?"

"What would be the benefit? He does not want to hear anything bad about Irene, so I will not be the one to tell him."

"I'm a good listener if you feel like sharing?"

She waited, sensing his unease. When he failed to respond, she touched the sleeve of his jacket. "This woman was special to you, *yah*?"

He nodded. "I loved her." He hesitated a moment before adding, "At least, I thought I did."

The reins twined through his finger. "Have you ever been in love?"

Becca thought for a long moment, wishing she could answer Zeke's question. Had she loved someone once upon a time? Did she love someone now?

She shook her head and sighed. "I wish I knew."

He took her hand in his, causing her heart to lurch. She turned and looked into his eyes, seeing empathy and concern. Perhaps she had not answered Zeke's question correctly the way her neck tingled. Could the strange sensations have something to do with love?

"Forgive me?" he said.

She raised her brow. "Forgive you for what?"

"For asking a question about your past when you have no memory. I should have realized my query would cause you more upset."

"I wish I could tell you about my past, but it is a total blank, like a clean whiteboard that has no markings. I try to see beyond the present and I get only a void. Still—" She squeezed his hand. "Tell me about Irene and your relationship with her."

He turned his gaze back to the road.

"Irene was pretty," he started to explain. "She knew I was interested in being with her and smitten enough to agree to anything she suggested."

"She suggested leaving the mountain and moving to town?" Becca asked.

He nodded. "Irene wanted to experience life. At least, that is what she told me. I asked her to be my wife. Hattie made a wedding dress for her."

"The pretty blue dress Hattie gave me to wear. It was meant to be a bridal dress." Becca's heart sank, realizing the upset she must have caused Zeke when she wore the dress planned for his bride.

"That was long ago, Becca. The dress should be worn instead of hidden away in a blanket chest."

"Seeing me in the dress must have upset you."

He shook his head. "Irene is gone. There is no going back."

"Still—"

"Still, you are not listening. Irene found an *Englisch*

man who spent money on her. Drug money earned from the sale of the methamphetamine he cooked up."

"Oh, Zeke."

"The chemicals he used were highly flammable. There was an explosion and a fire. Irene was in the cabin at the time."

"I'm sorry." Becca's heart ached for the pain Zeke had to have experienced.

Mr. Gingerich's words came again to mind. *You're a murderer*, he had yelled.

She turned to look at Zeke. Hard as the question was to ask, she needed to know the truth. "If that's what happened, why did Mr. Gingerich say you murdered his daughter?"

"I had been with Irene minutes earlier. She was angry, and I could not reason with her so I left and had not gone far when the cabin exploded. I ran to save her. I…"

His voice was thick with emotion.

"I tried to resuscitate her. She started breathing but died in the ambulance as she was being rushed to the hospital."

"Yet her father claims you killed her?"

"The sheriff told him what happened, but he does not have ears to hear."

Becca wrapped her arms around her waist and leaned back, her gaze on the passing darkness.

Was Mr. Gingerich a cranky old man who failed to accept the truth or did he know something about his daughter's relationship with Zeke that was better left unsaid?

Becca hadn't told Zeke about the knife she saw in her dreams. Was he holding back something about Irene's death, as well?

ELEVEN

Zeke was heavyhearted as he encouraged Sophie up the mountain to where Montcliff Studio was located. Becca had been quiet and lost in her own world since their brief discussion about Irene. Knowing she needed time to sort through the information he had shared, Zeke had remained silent, as well.

In the distance, he spied the two large soundstages that rose like giants against the star-studded sky. Floodlights illuminated the area and brightened the various buildings set in stark contrast to the dark night.

Becca sighed and finally spoke. "I don't have a good feeling about this place."

"I understand your concern, but Levi Gingerich said Caleb was working tonight. I want to talk to him."

"I told you the van with the Montcliff Studio logo must mean something to me, Zeke. Suppose I worked here as we talked about? If so, you're bringing me to the very place where I might be recognized."

"The sun has set, Becca. The filming is taking place in town. I doubt we will see anyone roaming about tonight, but to ensure you are not recognized, hide in the rear of the buggy."

"What if someone grabs me, Zeke? Larry Landers chased after me today. Other men have, as well. You must realize my concern."

"Yet you need to find out why those men were chasing you, Becca. That is what we are trying to do. As I said before, everyone is in town. You will not be discovered. Trust me."

Her frustrated sigh as she climbed into the rear told him that was the issue. She did not trust him, although he could not blame her. She knew nothing about her past and knew little about him, so she was smart to be wary. Zeke needed to earn her trust. Hopefully with time, she would realize he wanted what was best for her.

"We will not stay long," he assured her.

"Long enough to be found out," she muttered under her breath.

A man stood at the entry gate and stepped into the road as Zeke guided the mare forward.

The guard held up his left hand. "This area is off-limits."

"I am here to talk to Caleb Gingerich. He works in food service."

"Come back tomorrow."

Zeke nodded. "This is something I might do depending on what he tells me this evening. Caleb Gingerich asked me to deliver fresh pastries and breads to the dining area. I need to know when the order is to arrive."

Zeke hesitated a moment and then raised a brow. "Unless you want to cancel the order of mouthwatering pies and cakes."

"Look, I'm just doing my job." The guard shrugged and checked a clipboard he held in his right hand. "No one said anything about a delivery tonight."

"Not a delivery, but confirmation of an order." Zeke peered into the enclave, seeing a number of trailers and other temporary buildings. "Where can I find the dining hall?"

The guard pointed to the fork in the road. "Stay on this path. You'll pass the dorms that house the employees. Keep going straight until you come to a circle. The executive trailers and the office will be on the left. The commissary is directly to the right. The kitchen is on the far side in the rear of the building. You should find Gingerich there. If not, you'll have to come back tomorrow."

Zeke nodded his thanks and flicked the reins. Sophie's hooves clip-clopped on the pavement.

"He did not see you," Zeke whispered over his shoulder once the buggy turned at the fork.

Becca failed to respond, and he knew she was still worried about what might happen. "As I told you before, Becca. You will not be recognized."

"I don't share your optimism."

He glanced into the back of the buggy, seeing the faint outline of her oval face and the whites of her eyes opened wide with expectation.

"The studio looks abandoned. I do not see anyone wandering around the area. You can relax."

"I'll relax once we return to Hattie's house."

A circle of trailers appeared on the left. A sign in front of the building on the right read: Montcliff Studio Commissary. The front of the structure was dark. Rounding the corner, Zeke saw the well-lit kitchen. Caleb's red convertible was parked in a nearby lot.

Zeke pulled Sophie to a stop in a shadowed clearing behind a hedge of bushes. "Stay in the buggy, Becca. I will not be long."

After hitching the mare to a nearby tree, he hurried forward and tried the door. Finding it locked, he knocked and peered through the window, then smiled with relief as he saw Caleb heading toward him, carrying a mop in hand.

Caleb unlatched the lock and opened the door, surprise written on his face. "What brings you here tonight?"

Zeke glanced at the bucket of sudsy water in the middle of the room.

"The floor needed to be cleaned," Caleb said without apology. "Come in. How about a cup of coffee?"

Zeke shook his head. "I wanted to check on the cook's order. Is he still interested in what Hattie can offer?"

"Definitely. He'll cut a check for her once he receives the baked goods. Tell Hattie to work quickly. He's eager to receive her items as soon as possible, otherwise, I fear he might hire someone else."

"My aunt cannot be hurried," Zeke said with a smile. "But I will encourage her."

"Knowing the hungry people are anticipating her homemade baked goods might spur her on," Caleb added with a chuckle. "Filming will be in town this week. They're working round the clock for the next couple days to get done early. I'll head there in the morning. Why don't I stop by Hattie's house on my way? If she has anything ready, I can take it with me."

"That sounds *gut*."

Zeke started for the door and then hesitated. "Do many Amish people work at the studio?"

"A few men have jobs in the carpentry department.

They're the only Amish I've seen. Are you looking for employment?"

Zeke smiled and shook his head. "I just wondered, especially if Hattie delivers her baked goods here. Will she be the only Amish person at the studio?"

"No one will give her trouble, if that's what you're worried about."

"With the movie star gone missing—"

"I told you, Zeke, Vanessa Harrington is known to be temperamental. Although the sheriff is asking questions. Evidently someone notified them, expressing concern."

"Has anyone else gone missing?"

"Not that I know of, but then no one is as big of a star as Vanessa or as big of a problem. The leading man is well-known, but he's not a prima donna, if you know what I mean."

"Did anyone contact Vanessa's husband?"

"They talked to him, but he was clueless about her whereabouts. Law enforcement is waiting to hear from Mr. Walker, the producer, in case he had contact with her."

"And if not?" Zeke asked.

"Then the sheriff will open an investigation. They're calling this a missing person case, although from what I've heard, they're looking for evidence that might indicate foul play."

Zeke's chest tightened. "And if they find anything?"

"Some of the folks here think the missing person case could turn into a homicide."

"They think Vanessa Harrington was murdered?"

Gingerich shrugged. "People gossip about all sorts of things."

Just as Will Troyer had mentioned earlier today. Concern wrapped around Zeke's heart. He remembered Becca's bloody dress the night he had found her. He and Hattie had wanted to believe the blood was from the gash on Becca's head. Now he realized the blood could have been from another source.

Was Vanessa Harrington dead, and if so, could Becca be involved?

Becca huddled in the back of the buggy and stared into the night, aware of the sounds around her. From somewhere music played. A door opened and then slammed shut, and a man walked along the road, heading to one of the temporary buildings near the sound studios.

She climbed to the front of the buggy and peered out, hoping to get a better look at the man. He wore a baseball cap and had the collar of his jacket turned up, so she couldn't see his features.

Surely, he wasn't someone from her past.

After climbing down from the buggy, she sidled close to Sophie and patted the mare's mane. "Everything's okay, girl. Be quiet so no one sees us."

Becca peered around the corner of the commissary and stared at the row of trailers that sat in a circle around a central common area. One of the studio vans was parked in a distant lot. Again, she wondered about the logo. Did it hold a clue to her missing memory?

Turning her focus back to the commissary, she glanced through a large window into the kitchen, seeing Caleb and Zeke inside. As she watched, the two men shook hands, and Zeke opened the door to leave.

Grateful that she would not be alone much longer,

Becca turned her focus back to the trailers, feeling a bit of déjà vu flood over her.

Even from this distance she could see a sign on one of the doors that read Vanessa Harrington. The missing movie star. A small light glowed from within the trailer as if someone had inadvertently left on a lamp.

Footsteps caused her to turn as Zeke rounded the corner and hurried to where she stood.

"A few Amish men work in the carpentry department," Zeke quickly explained as he reached for the reins. "Caleb has not noticed any other Amish employees."

Becca grabbed his arm. "See the trailer with the movie star's name on the door?"

Zeke stared in the direction she had indicated. "Vanessa Harrington?"

Becca nodded. "Caleb said she's not here now, so no one would be inside."

Zeke shot her a questioning glance. "I have a feeling you want me to be a Peeping Tom."

She shook her head. "Peeping Toms look at people. I want you to peer through the window and tell me what you see."

"I will see furniture, maybe a rug, table and chairs."

"The rug, Zeke. Tell me what the rug looks like."

He stared at her for a long moment. "Is there something you have remembered that you have not shared with me?"

She sighed. "I'm not sure if it has anything to do with the movie star, but I've dreamed of a carpet with a geometric design. Do you know what a trellis pattern is?"

He pursed his lips. "Squares running on a diagonal?"

"I never thought of it that way, but yes. That's one way to describe it."

"So you want me to see if there is a trellis pattern on the rug? And you want to know this because you have dreamed about the pattern?"

"Twice."

"Why not go together?" He glanced around the central clearing. "Everything is quiet. Caleb said once again that the studio people are in town filming." He pointed to the wooded area adjacent to the star's trailer. "We can approach the trailer on the far side. The woods will provide cover."

"What about the buggy?"

"The hedge of bushes keeps it hidden from the main area. We will hurry."

He took her hand and they worked their way through the woods and approached the trailer located closest to the commissary. Zeke stepped toward the window and then motioned her forward.

Her neck tingled with apprehension when she glanced through the window and saw the area rug in the entrance foyer. Lime green trellis on a beige background. The pattern was identical to the rug in her dreams.

Except the rug in her dream was stained with blood.

A door opened on the far side of the clearing.

Her heart lurched when Larry Landers stepped outside.

Zeke grabbed her hand and they hurried back to the forested area.

"Hey!" Landers yelled. "What're you doing?"

Landers had chased her today. Becca couldn't let him find her tonight. She and Zeke ran deeper into the woods, needing to disappear. Just as before, branches grabbed at Becca's clothing and scratched her hands. Her foot snagged on a root. She tripped. Zeke caught her, and they stumbled on.

Her side ached. The last thing she needed was a cramp. She jammed her right hand under her ribs and pushed up, hoping to relieve the pain.

Zeke must have been aware of her struggle. He squeezed her left hand and guided her behind a large boulder. Collapsing against the rock, she struggled to catch her breath.

Holding his finger to his lips, Zeke motioned for her to be still.

She listened for Larry's footsteps, but heard nothing except her own ragged inhale and exhale of breath.

Had he given up the chase? Or had he stopped as well to study the terrain, searching for movement?

She envisioned him, ear cocked, listening for them to make a sound that would alert him to their whereabouts.

As the silence continued, she peered around Zeke and studied their surroundings. Through the trees, she could see lights from the studio enclave.

Zeke motioned that they needed to go deeper into the woods. Ever so slowly, they stepped away from the boulder and picked their way through the dense underbrush, stopping repeatedly to listen for the man's approach. At last satisfied that he was no longer behind them, they circled around the periphery of the studio and headed closer to the commissary.

Glancing through the heavy brush, they saw Landers standing in the clearing, hands on his hips, staring into the thicket where they hid.

The kitchen door opened and Caleb stepped outside. He called out to Landers, "Is something wrong?"

"Did anyone run past the commissary?"

Caleb shook his head. "I didn't see anyone. Why?"

"Someone took off running when I came outside. We've had a few things go missing recently. Probably a kid from town. This one wore a wide-brim hat like the Amish."

The door of a second trailer opened. Becca's heart stopped as another tall, muscular man stepped onto the stoop.

"What's going on?" he asked.

"Someone was snooping around." Once again, Landers stared at where Becca and Zeke hid.

She shivered. What if he saw them in the underbrush? She never should have come to Montcliff Studio. Something was happening here, and Becca was beginning to think she was involved.

TWELVE

Zeke's mouth was dry and his palms wet. He kept his eyes focused on the two men talking among themselves. The sooner he and Becca left the area, the better, but the men kept pointing to the woods.

He had not prayed, really prayed, since he had pulled Irene from the fire. That night, he had called out to the Lord to save her. *Gott* had ignored his request.

Tonight was different. He feared for Becca's safety. Gazing up into the night sky, he removed his hat.

Protect her, Gott. Protect Becca or whatever her name might be.

His father would not approve of his silent prayer, but then, his *datt* did not condone any of Zeke's actions.

Although Hattie did not understand Zeke's reason for not attending Sunday services, she never condemned him, for which he was grateful.

His aunt was a *gut* woman, and she had provided refuge for Zeke when he had needed some place to hole up and heal his heart. Just as Becca had needed refuge the night he found her wandering along the mountain road.

Zeke feared the men would remain outside all night. At long last, they nodded their farewells and went inside.

Still concerned they might be seen, Zeke and Becca remained in place for another twenty minutes until the lights in the trailers went out and the men appeared to have settled in for the night. Zeke hurried to the buggy while Becca remained in their hiding spot.

Not wanting the clip-clop of Sophie's hooves to disrupt any of the studio people, he grabbed the reins and turned the mare toward a dirt path he hoped would weave through the forested area and eventually end up on the main road.

Sophie responded to Zeke's whispered commands and the tug on the reins. Staying off the pavement masked the sound of her hooves. The only noise was the occasional squeak of the buggy. Slowly, he guided the mare toward the dirt path. He glanced over his shoulder, searching the studio grounds, to make certain no one had seen him.

He stopped, stood still for a long moment and studied the entire area, his gaze moving from the dormer buildings to the tall sound studios, standing back-dropped against the night sky, to the Montcliff Studio van and the trailers sitting dark in the night. Light spilled from the commissary windows and allowed Ezekiel to find a narrow path into the underbrush.

His shoulders drooped as much as his heart as he urged Sophie forward. He was responsible for Becca's safety and his carelessness had placed her in danger. The pain that swelled within him made him want to scream in anger, which was not the Amish way. What would his *datt* say? No doubt, he would admonish Zeke for not being able to control his emotions. Perhaps his father had forgotten about love.

Zeke shook his head, unable to see his prim and

proper father, pining for his mother—or any woman, for that matter.

Was Zeke pining now—pining and worried sick about whether he could get Becca out of danger?

As much as he did not want to admit his feelings, he was drawn to her.

"Zeke?" The brush parted, and Becca stepped onto the path.

Relieved to be reunited again, he opened his arms and pulled her into his embrace. She was warm and soft and fully alive. Everything that mattered most was with him at that moment and he never wanted to let her go.

Becca nestled into Zeke's arms feeling overcome with relief that the men from the store had gone inside.

He glanced over his shoulder, all the while urging her forward.

"We must hurry," he told her. "Come, we will walk Sophie farther along the path, then we will climb into the buggy and head back to Hatty's house."

The trail wound through the woods, and Becca wondered if she had run along that same path two nights earlier.

The moon broke through the clouds, which helped them make their way. She studied the path as they walked, looking for any clues or signs that she had traveled this identical route.

Something caught her eye. She leaned down and pulled a swatch of fabric from one of the low-lying branches and held it up to the moonlight.

Zeke stepped closer. "What did you find?"

"A piece of material. I'm not sure in this light, but it looks blue."

"Your dress was torn," he whispered.

She nodded. "If this swatch of fabric matches my dress, then I ran along this path."

Glancing back toward the studio, her stomach roiled. "What happened on that studio lot that made me run for my life and made a man chase after me?"

Tears welled in her eyes. "Oh, Zeke, what if I've done something wrong. You saw the trellis-patterned carpet tonight. The rug I remember was covered with blood. What did I do? Did I cause someone harm?"

"Do not think such thoughts."

"Look." She pointed to where broken twigs and trampled underbrush curved left. "This is where I left the path. We need to follow that trail."

Zeke took her hand. "Not tonight. It is late. Hattie will be worried. She thought we were just going to town, but we have been gone so long. We can come back tomorrow."

"You wouldn't mind returning? If we follow the trail, we might find something that would provide a clue as to what happened."

She shivered.

"You are cold. Let me help you into the buggy. Wrap yourself in the blanket. The road is not far."

Becca appreciated his help as he guided her into the buggy. She slipped to the back seat and unfolded the blanket, a crocheted lap throw, and wrapped it around her shoulders. As much as she would have enjoyed the warmth of Zeke's arms, she needed to keep out of sight in case someone else was on the path tonight.

As Zeke urged the mare forward, Becca glanced back to the fork in the trail. She would come back tomorrow. She had to know more about where she had been that first night. The torn fabric from her dress confirmed her presence.

What else would she find on the trail?

A section of bloodstained carpet? A knife?

She shivered again.

Or a dead body?

THIRTEEN

Becca and Zeke were both relieved when they arrived back at Hattie's farm. Just as Zeke had suspected, his aunt had been worried about their safety.

"I knew you would be concerned," Zeke told her, "but one thing led to the next."

Zeke explained about stopping to see Mr. Gingerich and his less-than-hospitable welcome. "He still holds me responsible for Irene's death."

"His heart has hardened," Hattie said with a disapproving shake of her head. "He was never an overly friendly man, but he was not one to jump to the wrong conclusions. The pain of losing a child has made him bitter. I understand his grief, yet I cannot condone his accusations."

"He told us Caleb was working at the studio tonight," Zeke explained. "We were close and decided to stop by."

"How is the movie star?"

Zeke chuckled. "He was mopping the floor in the kitchen."

"Hard work is good for a man, *yah*? His father spoiled him along with his sister."

Zeke's face darkened. Becca glanced away, realizing he still had feelings for Irene. Why would he not? They had planned to marry.

She thought of the warmth of Zeke's arms around her on the path and in the buggy as they rode toward Levi Gingerich's house. Some thoughts needed to be buried. She could not think of Zeke as anything but a friend who provided her safe haven and support.

Then she looked at his expressive eyes and the curve of his lips. Some memories lasted forever.

"You look upset, Zeke, that I would say this," Hattie continued, unaware of the turmoil Becca was feeling. "Yet, you know yourself Irene was self-centered. She got what she wanted when she wanted it."

"Irene might have been self-absorbed, but she had a good heart."

The older woman tsked. "A good heart if everything was going her way. She was not to be trusted, as your father told you."

"My father told me a lot of things I did not accept."

"The young have a mind of their own, it is true. Now, come, we have talked too much about the past. You are hungry, *yah*?"

Becca smiled. "I know I'm hungry."

"Wash your hands. The stew is ready. Pour coffee, Becca, while I pull bowls from the cupboard. There's fresh baked bread, as well."

Becca did as Hattie asked and after washing her hands, she filled three cups with coffee and set them on the table. Hurrying to the pantry, she smiled, seeing the loaves of bread along with the freshly baked cakes and pies.

"You've been busy, Hattie."

"Busy hands keep the mind from too much worry.

At least this is what I told myself. I wanted to get some baked items ready for the studio."

"Caleb said he will pick up anything you have ready in the morning." Zeke reached for a cup of coffee.

Becca glanced down at the trousers and shirt she wore. "Tomorrow I'll dress as a woman."

"I have a pale green dress that needs only to be hemmed," Hattie said. "You can wear that tomorrow. A different-colored dress might be enough of a change in case you see anyone throughout the day. If you go someplace in the buggy with Ezekiel, they will think you are courting perhaps."

Courting? Becca glanced at Zeke and felt her cheeks burn. He too looked ill at ease and glanced down at his feet, then turned to pour more coffee into his cup.

Hattie's comment must have caused him distress. If his heart was still with Irene, he would want nothing to do with Becca.

And what about her life? Had she been courted? Did she have a husband? Was that who had chased her through the woods?

Tomorrow, when they searched the wooded area, they might find some new clue to her past. Going in daylight, even though it was dangerous, might provide the clues she needed to unlock her memory.

"Caleb said the crew will be filming in town tomorrow," Zeke told Hattie. "That is why he is stopping here to pick up the eggs and baked items."

After they ate and the dishes were washed and returned to the cupboard, she opened a chest in the corner of the living area and pulled out a lovely green dress. "Come here, Becca, I need to see about the hem."

"I'll hold it up. You place a straight pin, Hattie, where the hem should be. I'll do the sewing."

"Are you sure?" the Amish woman asked.

"Of course. I've been sewing for years."

Zeke stared at her.

She turned to look at him. "I remembered something."

He nodded. "You remembered sewing."

She smiled, and a surge of relief swept over her. "Maybe going to town and to the studio was good for me. Something must have triggered my memory."

"Time has passed," Hattie said with a nod. "The trauma to your head is healing. This is *gut*."

Becca took the dress and the needle and thread Hattie handed her. She settled into a chair near one of the oil lamps and turned up the hem, and then started to stitch it in place.

She glanced at Zeke and expectation stabbed her heart. If only this was how her life could be, sewing by the light of the oil lamp with Zeke nearby.

Zeke watched her sew, leaning into the ring of light around the side table, and thought of how his mother used to sew or read by the light of the oil lamp.

Everything about Becca that he had seen so far indicated she was Amish. Which meant the feelings he had for her weren't inappropriate.

He let out a breath and settled into a chair near the wood-burning stove, enjoying its warmth and the inner glow he felt from sitting close to Becca.

He glanced at Hattie's Bible on the bookshelf. She read from it nightly and had worn the pages thin. Reaching out, he touched the leather cover, thinking back to when his mother was alive and the family would gather together in the evening to play checkers. *Mamm* would pop corn and the house would be filled with laughter. Before bed, his *datt* would read from Scripture, the verses chosen with care to provide a fitting end to a day of hard work and family togetherness.

The long-forgotten memory brought warmth to his heart. Looking into the future, he thought of evenings shared in similar ways with Becca.

"You are thinking of Irene."

Becca's voice was almost a whisper.

He glanced at her and raised his brow. "Why do you say that?"

"The smile that tugged at your lips. Much was said about her today. Your mind is returning to what you both shared. It is a good thing, Ezekiel."

He did not understand nor appreciate Becca's comments. His thoughts had not been on Irene. The way her life had ended was tragic and not one that brought smiles. Two years and he was still weighed down with the guilt.

Frustrated by the past and not knowing what the future would hold, he rose from the chair. "You do not understand, Becca."

Her eyes widened and pain flashed from her gaze. "Did I say something wrong?"

Without explanation, he climbed the stairs and headed to his room. The unlit oil lamp stood on his dresser, but he remained in darkness and stared outside into the night. The problem was Zeke and the mixed-up emotions he felt when he was around Becca.

He needed to know more about her before he allowed

this newcomer into his life. Would he ever learn who she was and where she had come from?

Becca's heart was heavy when she climbed the stairs that night. She hung the hemmed green dress on a wall peg near the blue dress Hattie had washed and returned to Becca's room earlier in the day.

Sifting through the folds of blue material in the skirt, Becca found the large tear. Pulling out the swatch of fabric she had found on the path tonight, she held it up against the torn portion of the dress.

The fabric matched perfectly.

Becca's heart was heavy. The path she had taken that fateful night had been from the studio, along the trail and then into the deep brush they would explore tomorrow.

Zeke had acted strangely tonight, which troubled her and sapped her enthusiasm for uncovering any more clues to her past. What if her memory returned and brought with it the terrible reality of what had happened that night?

Becca wasn't ready to find out the truth about her past. Not now. Maybe tomorrow she would be stronger and able to handle whatever she would learn.

Tonight, she needed to sleep without dreaming about a Montcliff Studio logo and a stained carpet and bloody knife. Tonight she wanted to dream about Ezekiel holding her in his arms.

FOURTEEN

Becca rose early the next morning, eager for the day to advance. The small revelation that she enjoyed sewing made her optimistic. Hattie had said the blow to her head was getting better and more of her memory would soon return.

Excited about her progress, Becca slipped on the green dress, enjoying the feel of the crisp cotton. The color was a favorite.

After pulling her hair into a bun and settling her *kapp* in place with hairpins, she raced downstairs, almost tripping over her feet.

"Hattie," she called. "I'm remembering more things."

"Wunderbar." Hattie greeted her with open arms. The women hugged.

"I told you not to worry," the older woman assured Becca.

She glanced out the window and saw Zeke in the barnyard.

"Fetch the butter and milk," Hattie requested. "We will eat soon. Zeke said he wants to box up the baked goods early to be ready for Caleb's arrival."

"I'll hurry."

Becca ran outside and waved to Zeke. He finished adding water to the trough for the horses and then approached Becca.

"The dress suits you." He smiled, and his eyes twinkled.

"Guess what?" she said, finding it hard to hold back her excitement.

He shook his head. "What?"

"My memory is returning."

The smile left his face and worry flicked across his gaze. Evidently he didn't share her exuberance.

"What have you remembered?" he asked.

"You don't look happy for me."

"I am glad you have remembered some things, but I want to hear what you have learned."

She pointed at the dress. "Green is a favorite color."

He nodded. "And you've learned something else?"

"That I enjoy sewing."

"You said that last night. Is there something new?"

Her enthusiasm plummeted. "That's all, but it's exciting, Zeke."

He nodded. "*Yah*, of course, it is something *gut* to know about yourself. But I thought you had remembered more important things."

"I will," she said with a forced smile. "Everything will come back to me."

She grabbed the milk and butter from the bucket filled with cool water and hurried toward the house. She wouldn't let Zeke's indifference temper her optimism. They might be only two small memories, but they were a start. More would come.

At least she hoped they would.

Before she went inside, she heard the rumble of

motor vehicles. The sound interrupted the peaceful stillness of the farm. Swallowing down the fear that grabbed her throat, Becca hurried into the kitchen. She stepped to the window and peered outside. A convoy of vehicles, all with the Montcliff Studio logo, drove past the farm and down the mountain.

She shivered. If her mind would stop playing tricks on her, she might uncover the reason for her upset.

After breakfast, Zeke boxed Hattie's baked goods and stacked them on the table. Becca washed the morning dishes and tidied the kitchen, then helped box the eggs so they wouldn't break on the drive to town.

"I want to meet Caleb," Becca told Zeke once all the eggs had been packed in the protective containers.

"Are you sure that is wise?" he asked.

"If Caleb recognizes me, then I will learn more about who I am. I need information, and Caleb might provide what I need."

"He has a good heart," Hattie said. "I do not think Caleb would do you harm."

"Then it's settled." Becca looked around the kitchen. "Do we have everything?"

"*Yah*, by packing the baked items in boxes, all of them should fit in Caleb's sports car." Zeke turned and smiled at his aunt. "The movie people will enjoy your baking, Hattie."

"This is my hope," Hattie said with a nod of her head. "If this first order pleases, I will make whatever more the cook needs."

"I can help you." Becca stepped closer.

"And I am glad for your help. After the *gut* job you did hemming the green dress, I will pull out fabric. We can start quilting."

Quilting?

The word brought to mind a small lap covering pieced with various shades of green fabric. Instinctively, Becca knew it was her quilt, one she had made when she first learned how to sew. The realization brought another insight into her past.

"My grandmother taught me how to quilt," she shared. "I remember a small quilt that was my first attempt. It was made of pieced green fabric."

"Oh, Becca, you have remembered something new." Hattie patted her hand and smiled with satisfaction. "Your mind is working again."

"If only it would work harder." Grateful though Becca was to learn about the quilt, she wanted the cloud to lift from her memory completely so she knew everything about her life.

Hattie's eyes twinkled as she turned to Zeke. "Soon we will learn that Becca lives on a farm not far from the mountain. She has an Amish mother and father and brothers and sisters who love her."

Becca wanted to share Hattie's optimism, but four men had chased after her. There was more to her past than a loving family. Someone wanted to do her harm. If only she knew why.

Caleb pulled into the drive and stepped from his sports car as Zeke and Hattie hurried outside to greet him. Zeke stretched out his hand, and the two men shook.

"Do you have time for a cup of coffee?" Hattie asked.

"Not today. But thanks. I need to get to town."

"Everything is boxed and ready for you."

Zeke ushered Caleb into the kitchen and introduced Becca. "She is visiting Hattie and offered to help."

Caleb nodded a greeting, but did not seem to recognize Becca. Zeke noticed relief in her gaze.

"The cook will love getting all the baked items," Caleb said. "And the movie crew will enjoy them, as well."

Working together, they grabbed boxes and loaded the items in Caleb's car.

Once again, the sound of a vehicle driving at a high rate of speed caused them to glance at the road.

Not a car but a black limousine.

"That's the producer," Caleb said as the limo raced past the farm and down the mountain.

"The man who left to find the movie star?" Zeke asked.

"That's right." Caleb nodded. "He couldn't find her. Vanessa's husband is claiming something has happened to his wife."

"But they had been separated," Zeke said.

"That's what she told everyone here. I'm not sure the husband thought the separation was permanent. From what people have said, Vanessa Harrington was fickle and flighty. No telling where she is now."

Zeke glanced at Becca. Her face was drawn. Was she thinking of the bloodstained carpet?

She stepped toward Caleb. "From what Zeke has told me, the movie studio only has a few Amish men working in the carpentry department. What about housekeeping? Are Amish women employed in that capacity?"

"That's contracted through a cleaning service," Caleb said. "Are you looking for a job?"

"If I stay in the area. I can cook and clean."

"Housekeeping might have an opening. I'll find out who you can contact and let you know."

"Perhaps someone has not showed up for work recently," she said. "I could fill in. Will you let me know if a position becomes available or if there is need for a part-time replacement?"

"I'll be happy to ask in town today. If I find out anything, I'll stop by here on my way back to the studio tonight."

Zeke walked Caleb out to his car and watched as he turned onto the main road. Had Becca remembered something more last night than her ability to sew? Had she remembered cleaning the studio? If so, that could be the reason she was concerned about the trellis carpet. Knowing about the bloodstains on the carpet could be the reason she had been chased through the woods.

After Zeke had tended the animals and completed a number of the other chores he had neglected since Becca had come into his life, he hurried into the house for lunch. The kitchen smelled of apple pie and fresh baked bread.

"More food for the movie studio?" he asked.

Hattie smiled. "And some for my favorite nephew. Wash for lunch. Today we will have cold cuts and cheese with the warm bread."

"Das smeckt mir gut," he said with a laugh.

"You are easy to please. By the way, Becca helped me with the baking. She is a gem."

Zeke poured a cup of coffee and turned at the sound of her coming down the stairs. Her cheeks were rosy, and her eyes bright. His chest tightened, and he almost spilled the coffee as he focused his attention on her.

"You have worked hard this morning," she said, flitting across the kitchen. "I am sure you're hungry, Ezekiel."

He liked the way she said his name. In fact, he liked everything about Becca.

"You wanted to explore the trail we were on last night," he said. "The day is cold but clear. I checked the almanac and snow is forecast over the next few days."

"For this, I am not ready," Hattie said as she sliced bread and placed it on the table.

"I have chopped enough wood for the stove and there is food to carry us through the winter." Zeke glanced through the window to the woodshed. "Snow will not be a problem."

Hattie laughed. "Perhaps not for us but the *Englischers* at the movie studio might have trouble navigating the icy mountain roads, especially if they do not slow down."

Becca filled a glass with water and placed it where she was sitting, then slipped into the seat as Hattie and Zeke did the same. "Exploring the trail would please me, Zeke. Again, I am grateful for your help."

His face warmed, but not from the coffee. He bowed his head to give thanks for the food they were about to eat, but also for the lovely woman sitting across from him.

Keep her safe, Gott, he silently added before he glanced up and caught her staring at him. For the longest moment, she held his gaze. Then Hattie started talking about a quilting the following day at the widow Shrock's home.

She patted Becca's hand. "I want you to go with me, dear."

"Would that be wise, Hattie?"

"Sometimes information can be learned as the ladies sew. Besides, I do not think the ladies in my quilting circle are the people who searched for you. We are a senior group, mostly widows. But we will decide tomorrow. A lot can change in a day."

Zeke knew how quickly things could change. As much as he wanted Becca to stay on the farm where she would be safe, he knew the importance of finding out about her past. In some ways, she seemed impatient, which concerned him.

Rushing too quickly into a situation could be dangerous. A lesson Zeke had learned. When he had found Irene, he had insisted she return home with him. In hindsight, he should have given her more time. Patience had never been his strength.

"Did you say something?" Becca asked once lunch was over and they were in the buggy heading up the mountain.

He had been silent since they had left the farm. "I regret what happened last night at the studio, Becca. It was not wise of us to go there."

"No harm was done."

"Still, I am concerned about your safety," he said truthfully.

"We will not go to the studio today, Zeke. You do not need to worry."

"But we must be careful and stay together. If I say we leave, you must climb into the buggy. Do you understand?"

"*Yah*, I understand." She glanced at the clear sky.

"We saw the buzzards flying overhead that first day. What was the reason for them?"

He shrugged. "A dying animal perhaps. Buzzards clean debris. It could have been anything."

"My dress had blood on it the night I arrived."

"You had a large lump on your head that was bleeding."

"Is it my own blood that I dream about?" She shook her head. "I don't think so."

"What else do you dream about?"

He stared at her for a long moment. "You will not tell me?" he asked.

"I dream of running in the woods."

"There is something else."

"Blood on a carpet, as I mentioned last night."

The hesitancy in her voice told him there was something more. Something she had not revealed. Something that frightened her or even worse, something she was not willing to admit.

The turnoff to the back path appeared on the left. "We must not take any unnecessary risks."

"I'll do whatever you say, Zeke, if that's what you need to hear."

What did he need to hear?

He needed to hear that Becca was an Amish woman who had been chased, but not because of anything she had done.

What if she had committed a crime?

He would have to walk away from her. Would he be strong enough? He looked at her pretty face. The way he felt, walking away from Becca would be impossible.

FIFTEEN

Turning onto the path unsettled Becca. She had been fine earlier. Now she was nervous and on edge. A sense of claustrophobia washed over her as the branches of the trees closed in around the buggy. She leaned back, wanting to climb into the rear and hide.

Instead she clenched her jaw, determined to face whatever they would find.

"The spot where we discovered the blue cloth is just ahead," Zeke said. "From there on, we will leave the buggy and travel by foot. I will hold back the branches so you do not tear your dress."

"Hattie was so good to give me this dress. She made it for Irene, didn't she?"

He shrugged. "My aunt wanted to make certain Irene had Amish clothing to wear once she came back to the mountain."

"Like the blue wedding dress?"

"That was a long time ago."

"Two years is not long enough to get over losing someone you loved, Zeke."

He pulled the mare to a stop and turned to look at

her. His gaze was heavy with emotion, probably sorrow for his love lost.

Becca wondered about her own past. Had she loved and lost, as well?

"I fell in love with being in love, Becca. I was young and foolish. Irene made herself out to be someone she was not. She told me we would live Amish after she had a little time to experience the outside world. I should have known the plain life would never make her happy."

"Did you think about leaving the Amish way, as well?"

"My mind was filled with all sorts of thoughts. Irene was not a lost love. She was a fickle confusion that happens to young men at times, especially young men who do not think with the wisdom of years."

"Stopping by her home yesterday must have brought back memories that made it seem so real again."

"*Yah*, it was real, but twisted and manipulative on her part, and a mistake on mine." He pointed to the broken twigs and the place where they had found the swatch of fabric. "The day passes. We must explore this area and then get back to the safety of the farm."

He climbed from the buggy and helped her down. She pulled the bottom of her skirt up just a bit and held the extra material around her knees so it would not snag on the branches.

True to his word, Zeke pushed aside anything that could scrape her skin or pull at her dress.

He went first, forging the way. The forest was eerily still as they trampled through the underbrush.

"I see a path of broken twigs, Becca. You were running through such dense bramble. No wonder you were scraped and scratched."

The memory of that night returned full force. Her heart pounded as if it had just happened today. She grabbed Zeke's hand.

He turned, concern evident in his gaze. "Are you all right?"

"Maybe we should go back to the buggy."

"We are close to the ravine. There is not much farther to walk."

"Ravine?"

"Did you not know? There is a waterfall and a steep drop-off."

"I heard water before I fell. Sometime later, I wandered along the road, but that's all I remember until I woke at Hattie's house."

"You might have fallen over the eastern edge of the ravine that winds down to the roadway below. That's where I found you. Had you gone farther up the mountain and more to the west, you would have come to the waterfall. There is a road that winds to the top, but also a path not far from here. The drop-off is dangerously steep. An *Englisch* boy fell from there some years ago. His body was never found."

She shivered, thinking of the dark night and not knowing which direction to turn.

"Perhaps the man who chased me was trying to warn me," she mused.

"Why do you say that?"

"I believe he told me to stop, Zeke. If he knew of the steep drop-off, he could have been trying to protect me instead of doing me harm."

"It is a possibility, yet something caused you to run in the first place."

He was right. She had run to get away from something or someone, no matter why the man had chased after her.

Zeke squeezed her hand and ushered her forward. She sensed his support and concern. Her fear, while still in the back of her mind, became more manageable.

Although thankful to have returned in daylight, she shivered again, thinking of her plight during the dark night.

"Here, Becca." Zeke pointed to a twisted branch. "Another piece of fabric, low to the ground. You came this way."

She reached down to retrieve the small piece of blue cloth and heard the distant sound of falling water.

Her mouth went dry, and she clutched Zeke's hand all the more tightly.

He shoved aside a large branch and pointed. "We are near the edge. Be careful."

She stepped into the partial clearing and peered down, seeing the sloping mountain and the large ravine down which she must have fallen.

"Stay back while I check the edge," Zeke said.

Releasing his hand, she struggled to control the fear that threatened to overtake her again. In her mind, she heard the man chasing after her and felt herself running toward the edge of the drop-off and then tumbling down.

Zeke approached the edge. Glancing down, he narrowed his gaze.

"What do you see?" she asked.

"What appears to be a roll of carpet that has lodged against one of the boulders far below."

Her gut tightened. "What color carpet?"

"It is hard to say. The backing is beige."

Could it be the carpet she saw in her dreams? If so, why was it on the side of the mountain where she had fallen? Had she seen the carpet that night? Was that the reason it kept playing over and over in her mind?

Instead of answering questions about who she was, the search through the woods was making her more confused.

She turned, holding her dress, ready to run back the way they had come.

"Becca," Zeke called after her.

Just like the night in the woods. She was running from someone again. This time she was running away from Zeke.

Zeke raced after Becca and grabbed her arm. "Everything is okay. You do not need to run from me."

She pulled in a deep breath, her eyes wide as she gazed up at him and then looked back to the edge of the ravine. "I'm scared."

"It is only rolled carpet. I have rope in the buggy. Stay here and I will be back in a few minutes."

"What do you plan to do?"

"I will go down the side of the hill to look at the carpet."

"It's too dangerous. You could slip and fall."

"I rappelled down the mountain often as a boy and called it sport. Besides you tumbled down that same hill as far as we know."

"I survived, but now I have no memory. This is not what you want."

She peered at the ledge again. "I walked out of this area somehow because you found me on the roadway.

Let's go back to the road and see if we can find a path that leads to the lower outcrop."

"I could lower myself without problem, Becca."

"And how would you get up here again? I could not pull you up, and I cannot drive the buggy. You would have to hike to the road and then climb up the way we came."

Realizing she was right, he guided her back to the overhang, and together, they studied the terrain below. "What you said is true, Becca. It looks like a deer trail leads toward the road. We might be able to come to that area without much searching."

They retraced their steps. The path Zeke had cleared earlier provided an easier way out, but they both sighed with relief when they arrived at the buggy.

The ride to the main road did not take long, and they soon found a turnoff and small clearing.

"I will cut a path for you, Becca. Unless you want to stay with Sophie."

She rolled her eyes. "You know I want to go with you."

He smiled. "I thought that is what you would say."

After tethering Sophie to one of the trees and satisfied that the buggy would not be seen by anyone passing on the road, they began their ascent up the mountain.

"There," he said, pointing ahead. "Do you see the trail through the forest?"

"A deer trail?" she asked.

"Probably. It is what I saw from above. The walk will be easier now. We will not have to worry about the bramble and branches."

Sounds of a car on the roadway caused them to turn.

Through the break in the trees, they saw the limousine racing up the mountain.

"It looks like the producer is returning to the studio."

"His chauffeur is driving too fast," Becca warned.

Zeke turned back to the path. "We must hurry. Some of the other movie personnel might follow the producer to the studio."

The deer path eased their climb and before long they approached the area Zeke had spied from above.

"Where's the carpet?" Becca asked, glancing around them. "It's not here."

"We cannot see it from this angle, yet we spied it from above. It must be close by." He headed toward a cluster of rocks. "Perhaps it is hidden behind some of those boulders."

She pulled at his arm and glanced up. "I can see the waterfall."

"It is positioned a little to the west, but you can hear the falling water. Someone stumbling along at night could easily have gone the wrong direction and headed toward the falls."

"You mean *Gott* was with me, directing my steps so I went to the best part of the mountain from which to topple?"

He nodded and smiled. "That is exactly what I am saying. It was *Gott*'s will that you survived that fall for which I am glad."

She squeezed his hand. "I am, as well."

"Now let us look for the roll of carpet."

They searched behind the nearby boulders and found nothing. Zeke was disheartened and looked up again at the rim of the ravine where they had stood just a short time ago. The carpet could not have disappeared.

"Zeke, what's that?" Becca pointed toward a stand of trees where the path continued to weave through the undergrowth.

"It looks like a continuation of the deer trail." He smiled and pulled her along after him. "You have discovered the problem. This first clearing is not the one where the carpet was laying. We must travel farther along the path."

They hurried through the dense trees until Becca gasped for breath. "You're going too fast. I need to rest."

He slowed down. "Sorry. I was not thinking."

"You were thinking of finding what we came to see." She pulled in a series of deep breaths. "Okay, I'm ready. But let's go a bit more slowly."

He kept her in mind as he led the way through the forest and was relieved when they exited into the daylight. He looked up, realizing this was directly below the place where they had stood.

"The carpet should be behind those boulders."

Hurrying forward, he nodded as he spied the rolled rug.

Bending down, he pulled on the stiff backing. "Is this what you've been seeing in your dreams, Becca?"

She gasped. "The green trellis design. The exact pattern I see in my dreams. If we unroll it, we should find a large bloodstain."

He tugged at the rope holding the carpet, released the knot and did the same with a second cord that held it bound.

Once the two ropes were free, he pulled back on the edge of the carpet.

Becca stepped closer.

"I don't understand."

They both looked down at the large spot. Not a dark black bloodstain. Instead, an area of the carpet was void of color.

"It looks like someone tried to clean the carpet with bleach that took out the color."

"The bleach took something else out," she whispered.

He leaned closer.

Becca's eyes widened. "It took out the bloodstain."

SIXTEEN

Becca's dreams about the carpet had been real, but without the bloodstain, there was no evidence to provide the sheriff should he become involved.

"Someone hurled the carpet over the edge of the ravine in the same area where they thought I had fallen." She tried to fit the pieces together. "Did they want my body to be found along with the rug or were they convinced no one would find either me or the rug?"

Zeke shook his head. "Maybe they hoped the sheriff would think you had fallen while throwing the rug over the edge."

"How could I have moved the carpet?"

"It is not that large of a rug." He glanced at the roll of carpet. "Probably six feet by eight feet in size. You could carry it, but it would have been a struggle. Or perhaps someone helped you?"

"The man chasing me?"

"It does not make sense," Zeke agreed.

"Nothing makes sense." She worried her fingers. "Now I'm even more convinced that something very, very bad happened to cause me to run scared that night. But what?"

"You were at the movie studio. You must know some-one there or you worked there."

"Perhaps Caleb will learn of someone from house-keeping who has not showed up for work these last few days."

A sound came from above. Zeke grabbed her hand and pulled her under the overarching ledge.

"What are you—" she started to object.

He covered her mouth with his hand, making her pulse race. She wrinkled her brow and pulled free of his hold.

He held his finger to his lips. "Shhh."

She shrugged and mouthed, *What?*

He pointed to the ledge above them.

Listen, he said silently.

She read his lips and turned her ear, struggling to comprehend what she was hearing. Voices?

A pebble fell from above, followed by a few more stones. Someone was standing on the ledge.

Zeke held up two fingers.

Two men? she mouthed.

He nodded, then pulled her back even farther.

"The carpet's still there," one man said. "Looks like the ropes binding the rug came undone."

"Which probably happened when we tossed it over the ledge."

"I told you not to worry. The cops will find it only when we want them to. First we need to stage the scene."

"I've got everything we need."

"Good. We can't have any mistakes."

The voices faded as the men left the ledge.

Zeke grabbed Becca's hand. "We have to hurry back to the buggy. Follow me, but don't make any noise."

She nodded and started after him. When they were almost to the forested area, she accidently stepped on a brittle branch that broke with a loud snap.

Her heart stopped. She turned and glanced up. A man ran back to the ledge. Tall, with disheveled hair that hung around his neck. His eyes widened when he saw her.

Becca remained frozen in place for half a second before she ran after Zeke and disappeared in the dense forest.

"Stop! I'll find you. You can't hide from me."

Hearing the man shout, Zeke guided Becca through the underbrush, his pulse racing. "We need to hurry."

The man on the ledge had seen Becca and would come looking for her. Could they get to the buggy and down the mountain in time?

They ran along the path, then slowed as they came into the initial clearing. Zeke glanced up and nodded before he motioned her forward.

Becca kept her eyes on the path as if she was worried about tripping and falling. Zeke did not need to tell her that sound carried in the forest. Any man-made noise would alert the men to their exact location.

Relieved when they arrived at the buggy, Zeke tied one of the carpet ropes around a tree set back about a yard from the roadway.

"The rope will alert us to the turn-off when we return." He helped Becca into the buggy.

"We're coming back?"

"If we need to retrieve the carpet for any reason."

He grabbed the reins and encouraged Sophie forward. Before guiding her onto the roadway, Zeke glanced up the mountain, searching for any sign of the two men.

Once they were on the pavement, he urged Sophie to increase her pace. He glanced back, relieved that no one was following them.

"I will tell Caleb about the carpet, in case the studio realizes something criminal has happened," he said as his focus turned back to the road. "The Amish do not usually get involved with the sheriff's office unless law enforcement questions them, but if the sheriff starts an investigation, they will need to know what we found."

"Law enforcement worries me, Zeke. If they are told, they might come looking for me."

"I will not mention your involvement to Caleb, so there will be no reason for anyone to draw you into the investigation."

"Do you think I am involved?"

"I know nothing at this point, Becca, and neither do you unless you have remembered something more."

She dropped her head and rubbed her hand over her brow. "If only I could remember."

"Caleb thinks you are visiting Hattie, which you are. He did not recognize you. He probably stays in the food service area of the studio lot and does not mix with those involved in filming except when they take their meals."

"Did I take my meals there?"

"An Amish woman might bring her own food, perhaps a bit of bread and some cheese or apple butter." He glanced back again to ensure the men had not followed them. "If you were cleaning the studio at night, you might have stumbled onto something they did not want you to see."

"The bloody carpet, but I don't understand why it was thrown in the same area where I was last seen."

"The men thought you had fallen to your death. Perhaps they planned to connect you to whatever happened."

"But how? And what about the scene the men mentioned? What do they plan to stage?"

"You remembered liking the color green and enjoying sewing. More memories will return before long. It will all unfold in *Gott*'s time."

"*Gott* does not listen to me. He listens to others, perhaps to you and Hattie, but he has turned his back on me."

Zeke nodded. "I feel the same at times. *Gott* listens to my father's prayers, but he turns a deaf ear to mine. Hattie has tried to convince me differently, yet I am still not sure. Perhaps *Gott* is not willing to help an Amish man who has made so many mistakes in his life. My *datt* said I would pay for my transgressions."

"Surely, he didn't mean that."

"He was hoping I would ask for forgiveness, but I am not ready to confess wrongdoing."

"You tried to save Irene's life. How can that be wrong?"

"I ran after her in my father's opinion. She was not Amish. Amish men only marry Amish women."

"But she had planned to return to the Amish faith."

"My mistake was believing her."

"Perhaps if your father knew what really happened?"

"He has ears to hear and eyes to read the news reports, yet he believes what he wants to believe."

"Like Mr. Gingerich."

Zeke nodded. "It is true about both men, although

they are different in so many ways. One is a bishop of the Amish faith, the other left the faith and made his own way being *Englisch*, yet they suffer from the same stubbornness and hardness of heart."

A sound filtered up the mountain.

"Shhh." Zeke held his finger to his lips.

He and Becca both tilted their heads to listen.

"Motor vehicles are headed this way," he said.

"What else is located this high up on the mountain?"

"Only the studio, but there is a turn-off just ahead, before the bend in the road. We will hide there." He flicked the reins. Sophie increased her speed.

Zeke's gut tightened. They needed to turn off onto the narrow road before the convoy came around the bend.

"Get going, girl," he encouraged the mare.

The sound of the approaching vehicles grew louder.

The turn-off appeared on the right. He pulled back ever so slightly on the reins and guided Sophie into the turn at a higher speed than he would have done normally. One of the buggy's back wheels raised off the ground for a second, tilting the rig at a precarious angle.

"Please, *Gott*," he prayed, fearing the buggy might topple over on its side.

The wheel dropped back to the dirt roadway. Relieved, he reined Sophie to a stop behind a thicket of heavy brush and tall trees. Peering from their hiding place, Zeke watched a van bearing the Montcliff Studio logo and two large trucks with the same markings pass by on the main road.

"We made it just in time," Becca gasped.

Zeke nodded. "They are returning early today."

Becky clasped his hand. "I'm glad we were on the

path before they passed. Something about the logo unsettles me."

"You will know more as soon as your memory returns."

"Oh, Zeke." Becca stared at him, her eyes filled with worry. "What if my memory never comes back?"

SEVENTEEN

After returning to Hattie's farm, Zeke settled Sophie in the barn and was walking back to the house when Caleb pulled his sports car into the drive.

"Can I offer you a cup of coffee?" Zeke asked as the younger man climbed from his car.

"I had one before I left town, but thanks." Caleb waved to Becca who hurried from the house.

"Did you learn the name of the housekeeping contact for me?" she asked as she joined the men.

"Susan Mast is her name, but no one filming in town knew her address. I called the housekeeping department and left a message. I'm hoping they'll call me back. If not, I can ask tomorrow at the studio office."

"Don't tell them who wants to know. I would rather find out more about the job first."

"Then I won't mention your name. If you decide you're interested, you can fill out an application at the studio office. Nicholas Walker is the producer. His trailer is in the executive circle, not far from the commissary. The main office is located in the trailer next to his."

"From what I saw last night," Zeke said, "it appears

that the studio plans to stay on the mountain for a period of time."

Caleb nodded. "At least one more film is scheduled. Although with all the structures they've built, I don't think they'll leave anytime soon."

"Have they talked about buying the land from your father?" Becca asked.

"I doubt he would sell. He may have left the Amish faith, but he is still Amish at heart, and the land means everything to him. That is part of his upset. He had hoped Irene would settle on the farm, marry and raise her family here. He planned to grow old surrounded by his grandchildren and cared for by his daughter and son-in-law."

Zeke saw the cantankerous old man in a new light. The plans he had for his senior years had been destroyed when Irene died.

"And what of you?" Zeke asked. "Did he not plan for you to farm the land?"

Caleb shook his head. "He has never seen me as a farmer and never taught me the farming ways for whatever reason. Probably because I was an awkward kid who made a lot of mistakes. My father lost patience with me and then became overly lenient and allowed me to do whatever I pleased. I needed a little tough love, but perhaps he was tired of trying to mold me into someone I was not. Some say I was a spoiled kid."

Zeke smiled, remembering Hattie had said that very thing just last night.

"You find that funny?" Caleb asked.

"My father claimed I was spoiled, as well," Zeke shared. "He said everyone in our generation is focused on worldly pleasure instead of faith and family."

"Perhaps our fathers do not remember when they were young. I understand both of them had more freedom than they needed. My uncle has told me stories about their escapades."

"Our fathers?" Zeke was surprised by Caleb's statement. "I did not know they were friends."

"In their youth, they were close. I am not sure what happened to drive them apart. Ask your father, Zeke. He might share more with you than my father does with me."

Zeke shook his head with regret. "You do not know my father if you say this, Caleb. Ever since he became bishop, he knows what is best for his youngest son. Perhaps he wears a mask of goodness, if what you say about his youth is true, to make up for the mistakes in his past."

"My father is the opposite. He wears a gruff mask, when inside he has a soft heart that has been wounded." Caleb stepped toward his car. "He's getting so forgetful these days."

"Before you go, I need to tell you what Becca and I found today near the waterfall."

"Something to do with my dad?"

Zeke shook his head. "Not your dad, but it may be tied to the studio. A piece of carpet discarded at the foot of the ravine. It appears to have been thrown from the overhanging ledge. A large area of the rug is void of color as if bleach had spilled on it. Do you know if carpet has been replaced in any of the studio buildings recently?"

Caleb thought for a moment before he shook his head. "I can't think of any furnishings or carpets that have been redone. Everything is fairly new so there would be no reason for any changes."

"It looks like someone tried to clean the rug," Zeke said, "and used the wrong product."

Caleb narrowed his brow. "I'm confused as to why it was discarded."

"I am, as well. That is why I wanted someone at the studio to be aware of what we found."

"You mean because of Vanessa Harrington?"

Zeke shrugged. "That came to mind, although as you mentioned, she is probably being temperamental and left to get her own way. Still—"

Caleb nodded. "Still it is a concern."

"Do not use my name, Caleb. After what happened with Irene, I do not want to get pulled into another investigation."

"I'll tell one of the managers and see what they think, but I will not mention your name. From what I've heard, they want to keep Vanessa's disappearance quiet."

"Yet they notified the sheriff's office," Zeke said. "I talked to a deputy when I was in town. Remember Mike Frazier? We knew him growing up."

"I saw Mike not too long ago. He's a good guy."

"He knew about the missing movie star but said no one filled out a missing person report."

"The studio wants to keep the information from the media. Larry Landers planned to distribute flyers once he got the go-ahead from the producer. Thankfully he still had them in his office. Mr. Walker returned to Montcliff this morning and wasn't happy from what I heard. He thought the flyers would have been bad publicity for the studio."

Becca tilted her head. "I don't understand what the problem would be."

"News travels fast, and a huge amount of money is needed to produce a film. The backers will be angry and rescind their financial commitment if they learn Vanessa has disappeared. It causes a number of headaches for the producer."

"Did Landers not realize what he was doing when he created the flyers?" Zeke asked.

Caleb shrugged. "He's a bit of a free spirit. I'm not sure how long he's been with the studio. I've overheard a couple comments about him having ties to someone with money outside of Montcliff, but I couldn't tell you who that would be."

"If you hear anything, let us know. We will deliver more of Hattie's baked goods in a few days."

"I should have mentioned sooner that the cook was thrilled with what she had baked and asked for a similar delivery day after tomorrow, if that gives her enough time. He put her check in the mail."

The kitchen door opened, and Hattie stuck her head outside and waved. Caleb repeated what he had told Zeke about the baked goods.

Hattie smiled broadly. "I am glad the items were well received. Thank you for delivering them today, Caleb."

"Not a problem, Hattie. Your check is in the mail."

"*Yah?* This is *gut*." She returned to the kitchen and closed the door.

Zeke extended his hand. "We must stay in touch even though our fathers have not kept their friendship going."

"I told you yesterday, I know you had nothing to do with Irene's death. I read the reports. You pulled her from the cabin and tried to resuscitate her. For which I am grateful."

"Perhaps someday your father will realize I am not to blame."

"I'll tell him again what really happened, although he may not listen. As we talked about earlier, it is a hard realization, but one he must face if he is to regain some sense of peace. Right now he is a bitter man with a broken heart."

Caleb patted Zeke on the shoulder. "You know about broken hearts yourself, but you have healed." Caleb glanced at Becca. "Life goes on, *yah*?"

"What you say is true. Life does goes on."

Caleb climbed into his sports car and nodded his farewell before he headed to the main road.

Zeke thought of Irene, musing how things would have been different if she had not died, but then he would not know Becca. Pulling in a cleansing breath, he felt a release of something he had held on to for so long.

He smiled at Becca. The past was over. It had ended the day of the explosion when the cabin caught on fire. Now he was ready to embrace the future whatever it held.

The afternoon and evening passed quickly, filled with work that needed to be done. Later that night after the meal had been eaten and the dishes washed and put away, Zeke struggled with a restlessness that confused him even more than everything that was happening at Montcliff Studios.

Becca and Hattie had retired early, claiming to be tired. Eventually Zeke followed them upstairs, but soon thereafter, he returned to the kitchen and then stepped outside to check the horses in the barn and gaze at the pastures and surrounding farmland.

"You seem anxious about something?"

He turned to see Becca standing in the open doorway to the kitchen. "I heard your footsteps on the stairs, Zeke, and expected you to return to your bed in a short time. When I didn't hear you, I got worried."

She stepped onto the porch. The moon was hidden behind the clouds, yet the stars provided enough light to see the remnants of the bruise on her forehead and her scraped cheek.

"Are you feeling all right?" he asked, still concerned about the blows she had sustained just a few nights ago.

"My health is fine."

"Perhaps you should have seen a doctor."

She held up her hand. "A doctor would have notified the sheriff. That is not what I wanted."

"You did nothing wrong, Becca."

"How can you be certain?"

"Because I know you. I know who you are."

She shook her head as if dismissing his comment. "You know who you want me to be. I don't even know myself."

Glancing up at the mountain, she shrugged. "Sometimes I stop and stare into the emptiness of my mind, trying to remember, yet it continues to fail me. I fear there is a reason I cannot remember, a reason that is so vile and heinous that my subconscious will not allow me to remember it again."

He stepped closer. "But that does not mean you were the one doing the vile act, Becca."

She stared up at him. "How can you be sure, Ezekiel? You are seeing me through the eyes of a man who has shut himself off from life. I stumbled into your solitude and awakened a part of you that you probably thought was dead. You have feelings for me. I can see it in your gaze. But your feelings are for a life that you are ready to embrace again. You are eager to leave your reclusive existence here. That is a good thing, Zeke, but it has nothing to do with me."

"Oh, Becca, you are so wrong. It has everything to do with you. You say that I was reclusive, but I went to town and interacted with the store owners and shop-keepers there. I bought and sold grain and livestock. I took Hattie's produce to market. I was not holed up here like a hermit."

"Yet your heart was closed, Zeke. You built a wall around your emotions, and although you may have in-teracted with people, you did not let them into your world, the private inner world you built for yourself."

She moved closer. "Did you ever read books about the knights of old? They lived in castles and went out to defend the king's land and protect the royal family. After the battles, they returned to the castle on the hill with the fortification, the moat and the stone walls that cut off those inside the castle from the rest of the world."

"I am not a knight, Becca."

"You are, Zeke. You're a good man who wants to pro-tect those you love. You take care of Hattie. You reached out to an old man who thought you were a killer. You did not try to change his mind because doing so would make him realize the failings of his only daughter. That is heroic, Zeke."

"You are looking at me through a fog and seeing what you want to see. You do not know me."

"I know you better than you know me."

"Becca—" He reached out and touched her hair that fell around her shoulders. "I do not need to know the Becca of the past when I know the Becca of this moment."

His hand circled her neck and everything within him wanted to pull her even closer. She had talked about the wall to his heart. If he had built that wall, he wanted Becca to step through it and to be with him no matter how isolated he was from the outside world.

"Do you know how beautiful you are?"

She shook her head. "That is not so."

"Of course it is."

"An Amish man does not talk of such things, and an Amish woman does not listen. Pride could swell within me, Zeke, which is not good."

"Not pride, Becca, but admission of the truth. You are beautiful. In every way. Not only your expressive green eyes and silky chestnut hair, but the warmth of your smile and the concern you have for others. There is so much about you that I want to explore."

The moon broke through the clouds and light played over her face. Her lips parted as if she wanted to say something, but then she stopped and everything in her gaze told him that she too felt the desire to draw closer.

Slowly and ever so patiently, he leaned in, his lips close enough to hers that he could feel the warmth of her mouth as if it had already joined with his.

Her eyes widened, she stepped back, leaving him empty and chilled by her rejection. She turned and fled back into the house, running away from him, just as she had done before.

Irene had left him for another man. Becca would

leave him because of her fear of the past. She could not accept today when she did not know who she was.

Was there someone else in her past who pulled her from him? Would he find her fleeing him again and running into the arms of a man she had loved before?

Where would that leave Zeke? Alone again. Broken. He would go back into the castle Becca had mentioned, but he would never again be able to venture outside the walls he had built to protect his heart. Not if he lost Becca.

Becca entered her bedroom, still surrounded by the nervous glow she had felt standing in the moonlight with Zeke. He had almost kissed her. The memory of his closeness warmed her from head to toe but also frightened her. What if she loved another man? Could that be?

She clutched her hands to her heart. Did the past matter when the present offered such promise?

Even if her memory never returned, she had today and tomorrow and the days going forward.

With her spirits bolstered, she almost laughed. Sleep would be hard tonight due to the promise of what life *could* be, no, *would* be in the days ahead.

Zeke had loved Irene, but he had told her more than once that Irene was in the past. Becca was here and now.

She twirled around the room, her full skirt billowing out. In her mind's eye, she imagined herself dancing with Zeke.

She stopped. Did Amish people dance?

Why didn't she know the answer?

There was so much she had forgotten and so much she needed to learn again. Surely with Hattie's and Zeke's help, she could master the nuances of the

Amish faith. Not knowing if she had been baptized, she would have to talk to Zeke's father. She hoped that would not be a problem, especially if she wanted to be fully Amish.

Again she smiled, thinking of Zeke's words. *Amish men only marry Amish women.* Was he assuring her of what the future could hold for both of them?

Her euphoria was short-lived as her mind started firing other thoughts so fast her head spun. The bloody carpet, the knife, running through the woods, and being chased again the next day and later in town.

How could she be dreaming of Zeke when such confusion surrounded her? She needed to think through everything she had learned so far.

If she had worked with the housekeeping department, she might have stumbled upon the bloody carpet. Someone could have walked in on her when she was cleaning that night and then chased after her because of what she had seen.

What about the actor in town who had grabbed her arm at the cattle auction? Was he somehow involved with what had happened?

If Vanessa Harrington had been kidnapped, a ransom would be demanded from her husband or perhaps from the studio, which could be the reason they wanted her disappearance to be kept quiet.

The men on the ledge by the waterfall had talked about the scene they planned to set. A movie scene or the scene of the crime?

She sighed and rubbed her hand over her forehead. If only her memory would return.

EIGHTEEN

Becca slept fitfully. The next morning she woke before dawn and hurriedly dressed and descended to the kitchen to help Hattie with breakfast.

"What is wrong, dear? You look like you did not sleep last night."

"I… I had a lot on my mind."

"Of course. Pour a cup of coffee. Caffeine will perk you up."

Becca feared she would need more than caffeine to brighten the day, but she dutifully retrieved a cup from the cabinet and filled it to the brim.

The first sip was bitter, but she forced another sip and then another as if the coffee had medicinal properties. Thankfully, some of the tension she had felt through the night eased.

"I'll get the butter and milk."

"Make sure you put on a wrap. The temperature has dropped."

Becca pulled a sweater from the peg by the door and hurried outside. Zeke approached carrying an armload of wood.

"Winter has arrived along with snow." His expression gave no hint that he had struggled through the night.

Becca smiled seeing the falling flakes. "I'll tell Hattie."

"I am going to town after I do the chores. I want to talk to the deputy about what we found."

"Yesterday you said law enforcement didn't need to know about the carpet unless an investigation was opened."

"According to the almanac, the snowfall will be heavy. I need to tell Mike Frazier what we found while we can still find the rug."

"But—"

"I will not mention your name, Becca."

"You wouldn't have been searching for the carpet if not for me. How will you explain that to the deputy?"

"Mike and I climbed the mountain in our youth. Exploring the cliffs and boulders was a favorite pastime. He will not think it strange that I found something on the ledge."

"If you're sure he won't want to talk to me."

"I am not sure of anything, but I will discuss the carpet with him and not the woman staying at my aunt's house."

"I'll stay here with Hattie."

"Do not forget the quilting she mentioned. I know it is important to her."

"She can go alone."

"Which is not wise. There is safety in numbers, *yah*?"

"Two women would not be much of a match for a couple of muscular guys."

"That is the reason I want you to go to the quilting.

The widow Shrock lives some distance from town. No one will look for you there."

Zeke took the wood into the house while Becca grabbed the butter and milk from the ice-cold water.

She glanced at the falling snowflakes and tried to imagine her childhood. She closed her eyes. For a split second, a scene flashed through her mind. She had come inside on a snowy day to get warm. Her grandmother had hot cocoa and homemade sugar cookies waiting for her.

The memory buoyed her spirits.

"I remember my grandmother," she announced as she hurried inside.

Zeke turned to look at her. "Just now?"

She recounted what she had seen.

"Such good news," Hattie enthused.

"I could see *Mammi* and felt her loving gaze. She had gray hair pulled into a bun and her *kapp* sat on her round face."

"Her *kapp*?" he asked. "Your grandmother was Amish?"

"Of course. Didn't you know I was Amish?"

"I thought this, *yah*, because of the clothing you wore when you arrived, but there were so many things you did not remember about the Amish way."

"The amnesia blocked it all from my memory, but it's coming back, Zeke. It's all coming back."

"You look relieved," he said.

"Relieved to have learned something new."

Hattie smiled. "Soon we will find that house where your grandmother lives."

"I was a young teen. A lot could have happened over the years. My grandmother could live far from here. My parents and I could have been visiting."

"Did you see your parents, as well?" Zeke asked.

She shook her head. "Not yet."

"The next memory. It will come." Hattie's eyes twinkled. "In the meantime, we are family here, Becca, and you are included, as well."

Becca warmed at the comment about family. It was true, she felt part of this household. If only she could truly be family. Standing in the large inviting kitchen gave her a sense of home and acceptance. She was drawn to Hattie's faith and her love for the Amish way and the plain life. Her habits of hard work and concern for others were rubbing off on Becca. She had started to feel that same sense of commitment to provide nourishing food and a clean and tidy house. After the vision of her grandmother, Becca felt even more at home in this Amish farmhouse filled with love.

She blushed at the thought of having her heart filled with love, as well. Love for Hattie, but also—was it love?—for Zeke. Such a good man who was concerned about her and her well-being. The best part was knowing she was Amish. Sharing that faith made all the difference.

"I knew you would start to remember," Hattie enthused. "*Gott* has brought you here to us for a reason, a very joyous reason."

Becca hoped the reason had something to do with Zeke.

Although nervous about meeting the older Amish ladies at the quilting, Becca was even more nervous about Zeke talking to the sheriff.

"Please don't tell Mike Frazier anything more than is necessary," she pleaded as Zeke pulled the buggy into the widow Shrock's drive. Zeke hurried around the buggy to help Becca and Hattie down.

"And be careful," Becca whispered to him, not wanting to frighten Hattie. "If the men on the ledge saw you with me, you might be a target, as well."

"I was well hidden in the woods. Besides, the *Englisch* think all the Amish look alike, with our matching clothing and black hats. No one will recognize me."

Still she was worried and stood watching as he rode out of sight.

"Come, dear." Oblivious to Becca's concern for Zeke's safety, Hattie motioned her toward the house. "With the snow, we are a small group today. You will enjoy the ladies and they will enjoy meeting you."

Hattie's comment proved true. The four ladies were delightful and made Becca feel instantly at home.

She enjoyed the sewing as well as the chatter that flowed all the while the women quilted. Little bits of news were spiced with laughter and shared along with the stitches.

"Mattie King has taken to her bed," Annie Shrock said. "Her daughter fears it is the flu."

"So many are sick now," another lady added. "Have any of you learned what happened to Susan Mast?"

Becca glanced up at the name Caleb had mentioned, the woman in housekeeping.

"Her husband says only that she is infirmed, but her daughter told my granddaughter that she had an accident coming home from work."

"At the movie studio?" another asked.

"*Yah*. She works at night. The roads are dark. It is not good for a woman to be alone on the mountain."

"We did not have problems before the movie studio arrived," Hattie said. Her four friends nodded.

"Did someone run her off the road?" came the question.

"This is what I heard." The hostess pulled her needle through the cotton. "Susan's buggy ran into a ditch and turned over. Evidently she was left for dead."

"How terrible."

"*Yah*. Her husband was worried and went looking for her, which probably saved Susan's life."

"*Gott* provides," an older lady intoned. Heads bowed in agreement.

Annie Shrock frowned. "I do not understand why her husband would not talk about the accident."

"He is a man of few words. Perhaps that is the reason."

"Perhaps."

Becca kept sewing and tried to keep her voice on an even keel. "Does Susan live close by?"

"Hers is the house that sits back from the road, just around the first bend when you travel up the mountain from here. You will pass the Mast farm as you and Hattie return home, Becca. You cannot miss their red barn with two silos."

The conversation switched to other people who were sick and to a woman who had given birth to twins.

Becca nodded at the news but kept thinking of Susan Mast and the buggy accident. Had she been run off the road as the quilter surmised and if so, why?

If the housekeeper had witnessed something she should not have seen, Becca wanted to talk to her. Perhaps she and Susan had something in common.

NINETEEN

Mike Frazier listened attentively to Zeke's mention of the stained carpet.

"Usually I wouldn't take the time to look at a discarded rug, Zeke, but you and I go back a long way. If you're concerned, I'm willing to check it out."

Zeke headed back to the mountain turnoff and waited until the deputy arrived. They parked on the road and hurried along the path he and Becca had taken yesterday.

Once they stepped into the second clearing, Zeke was relieved that Mike had agreed to come with him today. A heavy dusting of snow covered the boulders and ledge, and from the low cloud cover, it appeared the flurries would continue throughout the day, eventually obscuring the roll of carpet.

Leading the way around the boulder, Zeke stopped short.

"Where's the carpet?" the deputy asked.

Zeke shook his head. "It was here yesterday. Someone must have taken it."

"Who would want discarded carpet?"

"The person or persons who poured bleach on the

bloodstain and did not want the carpet found, Mike. It has something to do with the movie studio."

"How can you be so sure?"

"Because I saw the same trellis-patterned carpet in one of the movie trailers."

"I'm not going to ask what you were doing spying on the trailers. At least not now. I'll stop by the studio and have a look around."

Mike's cell rang.

He raised the phone to his ear and narrowed his gaze. "Yeah? Do you have a name? Larry who?" He nodded. "Landers worked at the studio?"

Zeke stepped closer.

"Did you contact the coroner?" The deputy paused as someone on the other end spoke. "I'm headed there now."

Mike pocketed his phone. "I'll talk to you later, Zeke. Go home and stay put."

"What happened?"

"That was one of the security officers at Montcliff Studio. There's been a death on the property."

Zeke's breath hitched. "Who?"

"Larry Landers. I talked to Vanessa Harrington's husband yesterday. He hired Landers to keep an eye on his wife. Evidently the job was too much for him. Landers hung himself and left a suicide note."

"Which could have been written by someone else," Zeke said. "If the movie star is missing and Landers was hired to watch out for her, maybe someone wanted Landers out of the picture."

The deputy tugged on his jaw. "You don't think his death was suicide?"

"That is something you need to determine, Mike, but if not suicide, then it has to be murder."

Becca and Hattie said goodbye to Annie Shrock and the other ladies at the quilting and hurried outside when they saw Zeke approaching in the buggy. Becca crawled into the second seat so Hattie could sit next to her nephew.

As soon as Zeke turned the buggy onto the main road, he told them about Larry Landers's death and that he had been working for the movie star's husband.

"The same man who chased after me in town?" Becca asked.

"The man who stopped by our house and wanted to film on our land?" Hattie added.

Zeke nodded. "Yes to both of your questions. He may have also been one of the men on the ledge when Becca and I found the carpet."

Hattie tapped Zeke's arm and then glanced back at Becca. "There is something neither of you have told me."

Becca explained finding the carpet and the two men talking above them on the ledge before adding, "As Zeke said, one of the men could have been Landers, although it is doubtful if he was working for Vanessa's husband."

"He was supposed to watch out for Vanessa," Zeke added. "Perhaps he became despondent when she went missing and took his own life."

Becca shook her head. "It does not make sense."

Noting the approaching bend in the road, she spied the red barn and double silos and tapped Zeke's shoulder. "Would you mind stopping at the farm. Susan Mast lives here, and I want to talk to her. The ladies at the quilting said she was recently in a buggy accident."

"The Susan Mast who works at the studio?" he asked.

"That's right. I want to find out if the buggy crash could have been something other than an accident."

Zeke pulled Sophie to a stop near the farmhouse. He helped Becca and Hattie from the buggy, and the three of them hurried to the door.

"Susan's husband is probably putting out corn and hay for the livestock because of this snow," Zeke said. "Perhaps we will find her alone."

No one answered their first knock. Hattie rapped on the door and raised her voice. "Susan, I need to talk to you. It is important."

A woman appeared at the window. Hattie smiled a greeting and pointed to the door.

Slowly it opened.

"I heard you were sick." Hattie pushed past the woman and stepped inside. "You know Ezekiel Hochstetler." She introduced Becca as a family friend.

Susan seemed unsettled and clutched her hands nervously. "I must ask you to leave, Hattie. I have not been well."

Becca stepped closer. "I worked in housekeeping at the studio."

Susan straightened her spine. "I know the people I hire, and you are not part of the housekeeping department."

Becca was taken aback by the answer. "You have not seen me before?"

"Never. Why do you ask?"

"Because your buggy was run off the road and someone left you to die."

Susan drew her hand to her mouth. "How did you know?"

"Something happened at the studio," Becca continued. "Vanessa Harrington is missing, and you have information that ties in with her disappearance, which is why you were attacked. They wanted to scare you. Or kill you."

Susan's shoulders slumped, and she nodded. "*Yah*, I fear you are right."

"Can you tell us what happened the night of your accident?" Zeke asked.

"I saw a light on in the office trailer. Earlier, I had received a note saying the office did not need to be cleaned, but I wanted to make certain everything was tidy. Just because someone did not want cleaning does not mean I could forsake my obligation."

She looked at each person as if waiting for their agreement.

"This is true," Hattie confirmed with a nod.

"Go on," Zeke encouraged.

"I had the master key and opened the side door, never expecting to see anyone."

"Who was there?" Becca asked.

"Two men. They were Hispanic and didn't speak English. They used hand gestures and signaled for me to go away and close the door."

"Why?"

"They were laying new carpet in the entryway."

Becca's stomach tightened. "What did the carpet look like?"

"It was the same carpet that is in each of the other trailers and the same as the rug that had been in the office previously. The rug had a beige background with a green trellis design."

The carpet Becca had seen in her dreams and on the ledge near the waterfall.

"I left work that night never thinking anything would happen. A black car ran me off the road. I was thrown to the ground and must have hit my head. The driver got out of his car and stood near me. I was too stunned to move. He called someone on his phone and said the problem was solved and that he had taken care of me."

Her eyes were somber as she added, "I believe the man thought I was dead."

"Hopefully we will soon learn who did this to you," Becca told the distraught woman. Hattie gave Susan a supportive hug before they left the house.

"Who wanted to keep the new carpet installation a secret?" Zeke asked Becca and Hattie as they headed home in the buggy.

"Probably the same men who are chasing after me," Becca said. "Only I managed to escape serious harm. To keep Susan quiet, they tried to kill her."

Hattie shook her head in amazement. "And Susan is fearful, so she holes up in her house, claiming to be sick."

"It's called intimidation and is against the law," Becca said. "At least, it should be against the law."

Zeke flicked the reins, encouraging Sophie. "Mike Frazier is at the studio now. He plans to stop by the house on his way back to town. Maybe he will have more information."

"What if Landers killed Vanessa and then someone killed him?" Becca mused.

"Or he could have taken his own life," Hattie said with a sigh.

Zeke nodded. "We will know something soon. Very, very soon."

TWENTY

True to his word, the deputy stopped by later that day. Not wanting to be seen, Becca hurried upstairs when his knock sounded at the door.

Hattie invited Mike in and poured him a cup of coffee.

He sat at the table with Zeke while Hattie busied herself in the kitchen. "Care for a piece of pie, Mike?"

"Thanks but no, Miss Hattie, although the coffee hits the spot."

As Mike took a long draw of the hot brew, Zeke told him about Susan Mast and her buggy accident. "Perhaps you should stop there on your way back to town." Zeke provided the address.

"I appreciate the information."

"What about Larry Landers's death?" Zeke asked. "Are you still calling it a suicide?"

"We're investigating, that's all I can tell you now. I did find some information in his trailer that was interesting."

The deputy opened the notebook he had placed on the table. "Landers was onto something that no one else has mentioned at the studio."

Zeke leaned closer.

"Landers thought a second person had gone missing, although when I questioned the human resources department, they claimed the person had given her notice and had planned to stop working within the week, which might be the reason no one seemed concerned about another missing woman."

Zeke glanced at Hattie and then turned his attention back to the deputy.

"Landers compiled some information on the woman. The gal comes from a dysfunctional home. Her mother has a record and is currently serving time."

"Her mother is in jail?" Hattie asked.

"That's right. The woman doesn't have a record, but my guess is she's probably been involved in some shady deals if her mother was in so much trouble."

"Which might not prove true," Zeke noted.

"I see a lot in this job, Zeke. It's hard to find a good apple on a rotten tree, if you get my drift."

"What are you saying?" Hattie asked.

"I'm saying we've got another missing woman who may have something to do with Vanessa Harrington's disappearance. Landers printed a missing person flyer on the movie star and then made a second flyer on the other missing person."

His phone rang.

"Excuse me while I take this." Mike scooted back from the table and stepped toward the stairwell.

Hattie's eyes were wide as she stared at Zeke. He shook his head ever so slightly. Neither of them needed to say anything to the deputy about the woman upstairs. Not yet. Not until they knew more about what had happened.

"Yeah, did you find anything?" Mike nodded. "Good fortune was on our side for a change. Run the prints through the database." He glanced up the stairwell and nodded again. "I'll meet you at the office."

Frazier returned to the table. "Thanks for the coffee, Hattie. I need to get back to town. Looks like everything is falling into place."

He pocketed his phone. "A couple of guys spotted a body in the river south of town. Evidently it was hung up on a downed tree."

"Vanessa Harrington?" Zeke asked.

"Appears to be her. She'd been stabbed multiple times." He picked up his notebook. "We found what we think is a murder weapon in one of the dorm rooms at the studio. A hefty letter opener covered with what looks like dried blood. The forensic guys will check it out. It's got the studio logo on the handle. One of the deputies lifted prints, then found what appear to be similar prints on the furnishings in the room."

Zeke rose from the table. "Are you saying someone at the studio killed Vanessa?"

"It looks that way. Funny to leave the murder weapon behind. But then, she left her belongings, although she didn't have much. We found the letter opener wrapped in a small green lap quilt. Looks old. Maybe something from her youth."

Hattie gasped.

The deputy glanced out the window. "That snow's piling up. I need to get going."

He started for the door and then turned back. "I almost forgot. I wanted to give you folks a copy of the missing person flyer Landers created on the second woman. Not too many people live this high on the mountain. Doubt you'll come to town soon with the bad weather. I wanted you to be on the lookout in case she appears in this area."

Zeke's pulse raced as he took the paper from Mike's outstretched hand.

"I'll let myself out. You folks have a good night and be careful if you see this woman. When I first learned of her disappearance, I thought it was coincidental, but finding the letter opener in her room makes her a person of interest in a murder investigation. She could be a killer. Pretty as she is, but, we all know, looks don't mean a thing."

He opened the door, and a blast of cold air swirled into the kitchen. Zeke glanced at Hattie, who bit her lip and shook her head. He lifted the paper and glanced at the picture in the center of the page.

His world rocked.

Without saying a word, he placed the paper on the table and then grabbed his coat and hat and headed to the door. "I'll be in the barn, Hattie. Don't hold dinner. I've lost my appetite."

Becca stood at the top of the stairs and heard portions of the conversation below. Closing her bedroom door behind her, she ran to the window and saw the deputy drive off, then watched as Zeke hurried to the barn.

Hattie climbed the stairs. The look on her face scared Becca when she pulled the door open.

"You heard?" the older woman asked.

"I heard enough."

"You need to see what the deputy gave Zeke. He is upset. I must check on him."

Tears burned Becca's eyes. She took the paper from Hattie's outstretched hand.

"No matter what Zeke says, dear, you can stay here until all this blows over."

Hattie left the room and hurried down the stairs.

A lump filled Becca's throat. How could a movie star's murder and a man's suicide blow over? Did Hattie really want her to stay?

Becca's heart hitched. Ezekiel had left the house. No doubt, he did not want to see her again.

Her mouth went dry. She glanced at the paper and homed in on the photo.

Her world came to an abrupt halt.

She studied the likeness of the woman in the picture—chestnut hair, green eyes, a slender nose, high cheekbones, full lips—then searched for a mirror, knowing full well she would not find one in this Amish house.

Stepping to the window, she stared into the glass, seeing the faint outline of her reflection. If only she could see her own face more clearly...chestnut hair, green eyes, slender nose and full lips.

A tearful lament issued from deep within her, gut-wrenching in its intensity as she realized the truth the flyer revealed.

Raising her hand, she touched the glass. The photo was identical to the woman staring back at her from the windowpane.

Becky Taylor was the name printed under the photo. She wasn't Becca Troyer, an Amish woman. She was Becky Taylor, an *Englischer* who had gone missing.

How could she have been so mistaken? Everything she had felt over the last few days since coming into this home had proved she was Amish, yet it was all a lie.

An Amish man can only marry an Amish woman.

Zeke couldn't marry her. He couldn't marry anyone who was *Englisch*. Plus Mike Frazier considered her a murder suspect because the letter opener, which she had thought was a bloody knife, had been found wrapped in her green quilt.

Who was Becky Taylor? The daughter of a convict, an *Englischer*, according to what the sheriff's deputy had said. Becca had wanted her memory to return, but now she was glad she couldn't remember all the terrible details of her past life.

No matter what Hattie said, Becca needed to leave the area. Staying on the farm would only cause Zeke and Hattie more upset, which she never wanted to do. Leaving Amish Mountain would be hard, but the hardest part would be leaving Zeke. Never seeing Zeke again would break her heart.

Zeke closed his ears to Hattie, but the sweet woman continued to defend Becca and encouraged Zeke to talk to her. "Things can be worked out," his aunt insisted. "Becca is not a killer."

Which was what Zeke wanted to believe. The initial shock of learning Becca was a missing *Englisch* woman and a possible murder suspect had made him unable to think clearly. Hattie's calm assurance that Becca was the same woman whether her name was Troyer or Taylor had brought him back to his senses.

Surely the murder weapon had been planted in her dorm room at the studio. Was that the scene the men on the ledge had mentioned they needed to create?

"She was upstairs earlier, Zeke. Becca needs to know that everything is all right."

Hattie's words played over in his mind as he and his aunt entered the kitchen.

"Becca?" Hattie called from the foot of the stairs.

Failing to hear a reply, Hattie glanced at Zeke, concern covering her round face.

"I'll check on her," he said, climbing the stairs two at a time.

If Becca had overheard his conversation with the deputy, she would be frightened. He had to reassure her.

"Becca?" He stopped at the top of the stairs, seeing her closed bedroom door.

Needing to ensure she was okay, he tapped on the door. "Becca, it is Zeke. Are you all right?"

He tapped again.

His heart pounded. All sorts of scenarios played through his mind about why she was not responding. None of them were good.

He pushed open the door, then peered inside, prepared to see her strewn across the bed with tearful eyes.

What he found sent a jolt of fear into his heart.

Her black bonnet and cape were gone. So was Becca.

The missing person flyer Mike Frazier had provided lay crumpled on the floor.

He picked it up. His gut tightened seeing Becca's photo. How could she be involved in a movie star's murder?

The name printed under the photo was Becky Taylor, but the woman in the picture was Becca Troyer, a beautiful Amish woman who had worked her way into his heart.

He had lost Irene. He could not lose Becca.

He ran back downstairs and hurried out the front

door, knowing he or Hattie would have seen Becca if she had left through the kitchen.

"Becca," he screamed.

He turned to glance in all directions, studying the winter terrain, hoping to catch sight of an Amish woman in a green dress and black cape. He saw nothing, and his heart nearly stopped when his gaze fell on the path into the woods. She had run away like she had done the night he had found her in the woods. Was her amnesia merely a way to hide the truth about who she was?

He did not care about her past. All he cared about was her present.

"Becca," he shouted as he ran into the woods.

He had to find her. He had to find her before someone from the studio found her first. She was running away again, running from her past. Only this time, she was running away from Ezekiel and that cut his heart in two.

TWENTY-ONE

Becca fought back tears until she could hold them in no longer. They spilled down her cheeks and clouded her vision so that she couldn't see the trail. Struggling to control her emotions and needing to keep moving forward, she pulled a handkerchief from the waistband of her dress where she had tucked it this morning and wiped her cheeks.

Imagining footsteps, she looked back. The forest seemed to be closing in around her, like that terrible night when she had run scared.

She was running scared again, but for another reason. Her mind was playing tricks on her. She envisioned Mike Frazier at Hattie's house, climbing the stairs and pounding on the bedroom door, demanding to arrest Becca.

Would he call her Becky? Was that truly her name?

She had to get off Amish Mountain and this rural area and make her way to another place where no one would find her. But she had no money and no way to leave. She tugged at her bonnet with frustration and wanted to cry all the more.

Yesterday, she had returned to Hattie's farm and had

found it filled with love. That was the reason she had to leave. She couldn't let anything happen to Hattie and Zeke. They were both so special to her and such good people with loving hearts.

So different from who she must be.

She hated amnesia, hated that she had tumbled down a steep incline and hurt her head. Sometime that night she had lost her memory.

Her life had changed just as it had changed when she had overheard the deputy telling Zeke about the letter opener wrapped in her quilt. Mike Frazier's revelation about the murder weapon only compounded the pain she had felt when she learned the truth of who she really was.

Her head throbbed thinking of what she had found out about herself. She was an *Englisch* woman who somehow was associated with the death—the murder— of a movie star.

Becca shivered. The temperature was dropping. She pulled the cape around her arms and ducked her chin into the neck of her cape. She had to think of her own safety and where she could hunker down out of the wind and snow.

"Oh God, or *Gott* as Zeke says, I'm lost and alone and frightened. Help me, Lord. Please. Help me."

All too soon, Zeke realized searching for Becca was like trying to find a grain of sand in a bed of gravel. He retraced his steps back to the barn and harnessed Sophie to the buggy.

Hattie hurried out of the house. "What happened? Did you find her?"

He shook his head. "She could be anywhere, although most likely, she took the path that leads up the mountain. If she left by the front door and rounded the outbuildings, the path would be the logical direction to go to ensure we did not see her."

"Why, Zeke? Why did she run away?"

"She heard us talking to Mike Frazier. Learning she was *Englisch* and a person of interest in a murder case had to be upsetting. Perhaps she feared we would reveal her presence to Mike."

"I feel responsible," Hattie said with a moan. "I gave her the missing person flyer."

"And I did not offer her support. Instead I ran to the barn to sort through my own thoughts."

"Where could she go?" Hattie lamented. "She does not know the mountain and so few folks live in this area."

"She is not thinking clearly and instead is reacting out of fear."

"The temperature is dropping. Tonight will be bitterly cold, especially for a woman wearing only a wool cape. You have to find her, Zeke."

"Pray that *Gott* leads me to her."

"I have been praying." Hattie grabbed his arm. "You need to pray too."

"*Gott* does not listen to me."

"You feel that way because of what happened to Irene. *Gott* heard your prayer, but Irene had closed the Lord out of her life. The problem was not you, Zeke. The problem was Irene." Hattie rubbed her hand over his shoulder. "You did everything right."

"Except I could not save her. In fact, I am responsible for her death, just as her father insists."

"*Ach*. Do not say such foolish things."

"It is true, Hattie. I went to the cabin to convince her to come back to Amish Mountain, but what I saw sickened me. She was burning scented candles, but the smell of acetone and other chemicals soured my stomach. Irene was high on drugs and threatened to ignite some chemicals used in making meth. I told her she had her own life to live, but what I needed and wanted was living Amish with or without her. I walked away never expecting her to act on her threat. She screamed for me to stay with her, but I did not look back…until the explosion and subsequent fire that quickly engulfed the cabin. I was still nearby but could not save her in time."

"You cannot carry such guilt, Ezekiel, when Irene was the problem."

"Do you not understand, Hattie, why I am to blame? I left Irene that day. She could not take the rejection. Whether she purposely caused the explosion, I will never know, but it was a reaction to my rejection."

"Oh, Zeke, you have blamed yourself all this time. Irene made her choice when she left Amish Mountain and took up with the drug dealer. She rejected you and the Amish way. Seeing you walk out of her life meant she was not getting what she really wanted. Irene's death was due to the choices she made not to anything you said or did."

Hattie gazed lovingly into his eyes. "Do you understand, Zeke?"

"Right now, I cannot dwell on the past. I have to save Becca. If anything happens to her—"

He could not finish the statement, but he was sure Hattie could read the dread that filled his heart. If anything happened to Becca, he could not go on.

"You will find her, Zeke. *Gott* will lead you to Becca."

If only Hattie's words would prove true.

He climbed into the buggy and flicked the reins, then flicked them again, hurrying Sophie along the drive.

"Find Becca," Hattie called out to him as he turned onto the main road. "And bring her home."

TWENTY-TWO

Becca ran until she could run no longer. Her side ached, and she gasped for air. Slowing to a walk, she rubbed the stitch in her side and kept moving along the trail, not sure where she was headed.

Thinking back to the time in the buggy with Zeke, she tried to remember seeing other Amish homes that might provide food and water and someplace safe to stay for the night. She needed time to decide where she would go and how she would get there.

On the trip to town, they had passed homes, but none were close to Hattie's farm. Plus, the path she was on lead up the mountain, not toward town.

She rubbed the back of her neck, realizing her own foolishness. Much as she didn't want to be alone on the mountain, she couldn't stay at Hattie's farm. The deputy would have found her. He would have arrested her and taken her to jail for the murder of Vanessa Harrington.

She shivered at the thought of being hauled away to jail and imagined looking back to see Ezekiel and Hattie standing in front of the house as the deputy's sedan disappeared from sight with her handcuffed in the rear.

Instead of being hauled away, she had made a decision to save herself and thus save Hattie and Zeke. They would not understand, but she couldn't stay there on the farm and draw shame on them. Still, she wished she was anywhere but on this lonely path not knowing where she was headed.

The sound of voices startled her. Her heart lurched, and she stopped to listen, trying to get some sense of where the sound was coming from. She scurried farther along the path and up a small rise to a clearing. Hunching down, she peered over the rise and studied the surrounding countryside.

Suddenly she grimaced. She knew where she was and it wasn't good, but at least, she had stumbled upon another house. Just not one that might offer sanctuary.

Peering over the rise again, she saw Mr. Gingerich standing forlorn on his driveway, talking to himself.

"What are you doing out here, Dad?" Caleb raced out of the house. "You'll catch a cold."

"I'm thinking about the studio. Those folks think they can push me around, but they can't. I own the land and I'm not about to let them buy even one square foot of property. They can continue to rent, as long as they give me what I need. A sizable monthly rent check and access to the property."

"The only place you've gone recently is to the doctor in town, Dad. You don't need access to the movie studio."

"Maybe not, but I want to make sure they're not hurting my land."

Caleb shook his head. "Come on, Dad. Let's head back to the house. I have to return to the studio and talk to one of the managers. Promise me you'll stay inside until I get back."

"All right, but I'm not about to let anyone tell me what to do."

"Have I ever told you what to do?" Caleb asked.

"Reckon you haven't. Fact is, you've been a good son, although I've failed to tell you that too many times. I like having you with me. If your sister were still alive I would be a happy man."

"You can choose to be happy even though Irene is gone. People survive. It's painful and hurts, but you're strong, Dad. You can go on."

"Maybe I can survive, but some days I don't want to make the effort."

"I need you, Dad. Don't leave me."

The old man put his hand on his son's shoulder and the two of them walked toward the house.

Although she was glad the father and son had reconciled, Becca needed to find shelter. The barn door stood open. Once the men were inside the house, she entered the barn.

The stalls were empty, but the wooden structure still smelled of horses and feed. A tractor sat near the door. No doubt, when Mr. Gingerich turned *Englisch*, he had forsaken the horse for the engine.

Becca touched the cold steel tractor, thinking of the difference between living plain and fancy. Wherever she ended up, she wanted it to be an Amish community where she could focus on the simple pleasures of life. *Gott* had answered her prayer in the woods and had brought her to this protective hideaway.

Thanks to Hattie's deep faith, Becca was beginning to see that her problems had nothing to do with *Gott*'s lack of concern and understanding, but more her own lack of faith. Over time, she hoped—no, she prayed—

her faith in *Gott* would grow stronger. No matter what had happened to her in the past, she needed the Lord now.

In the rear of the barn, she found bales of hay that would provide a place for her to rest and a horse blanket in the tack room that would keep her warm.

Peering out at the house, she saw no one and scooted through a back door to the empty paddock. Ignoring the chickens who perched in the nearby henhouse, she pumped water into a tin cup, rinsed it clean, then refilled it and drank deeply.

Just as before, *Gott* had provided.

If only both Gingerich men would stay inside and not come to the barn. The possibility of not being interrupted over the next few hours until she could form a plan gave Becca hope.

She grabbed the blanket and wrapped it around her head and shoulders, appreciating the warmth, and stretched out on the hay bale. The smell of the dried grass was strong and made her drowsy. Closing her eyes, she wondered about her roots, whether they were agricultural and rural, or urban. What had she done in her former life? Probably not found shelter in a barn cuddled up on a bale of hay.

She drifted to sleep and woke with a start sometime later to the sound of raised voices.

Thoughts of the deputy who had stopped at Hattie's farm came to mind, but when she threw the covering aside and peered through a small crack in the barn door, she was more confused than ever.

Caleb's car was gone, and Mr. Gingerich stood in the driveway arguing with someone whose back was to Becca. He wore a dark-colored hoodie pulled over his head, along with jeans and work boots.

The roar of her pulse sounded in her ears, making it difficult to hear what the two men were saying. She strained to see what was happening, then turned her ear toward the opening in the barn, hoping to pick up at least a portion of the heated discussion.

The sound of a fistfight made her stomach tighten. She leaned closer to the opening and spied Mr. Gingerich stagger back, his hand raised to his jaw.

The man who had struck him appeared in view and leveled a second blow, then another. With each punch, Becca grimaced, feeling the pain as the attacker continued to pummel the older man with his fists.

"Tell me what you know," the attacker demanded.

"I won't tell you anything." The older man struggled to maintain his balance. He raised his fists and refused to back down.

Becca searched the barn and found a pitchfork.

Peering from the barn, she saw Mr. Gingerich lay sprawled on the ground. The attacker knelt over the old man, his fist raised to strike again.

She slipped out the door, ran full steam toward the assailant and jabbed the pitchfork into his right thigh.

He screamed with pain, grabbed the handle and ripped it from her hands. With a fierce growl, he struck her with the back of the heavy steel tines.

She fell to the ground.

He kicked her side. She gasped.

The guy grabbed her arm and jerked her upright.

She struggled to free herself from his hold. "Let me go."

"Becky?" His eyes narrowed. "How'd you get here?"

Becky? She blinked, seeing the man who had chased her into the bull pasture. Shaggy beard, beady eyes and unkempt hair pulled into a man bun.

"I'm protecting an old man from you. You're despicable. Pick on someone your own age."

He looked confused. "Don't you recognize me? It's Kevin Adams." His voice softened ever so slightly as if he was trying to either assuage her anger or his. "The movie star. We're friends. Remember?"

The only thing she remembered was they weren't friends.

He smirked. "Everything will work out, hon, the way I said it would. Vanessa's gone so you can take her part in the next movie."

Her stomach soured. "I'm not your hon," she insisted. "I'm Becca Troyer."

"You're taking this Amish role too far. Cut it out, Becky. You made the costume and told me you felt Amish when you put it on, but you've got to end this foolish notion to actually become Amish."

"I don't know what you're talking about."

"Nicholas Walker—the producer—planned to fire Vanessa and give you a part in the film."

"I don't remember."

"Of course, you do. That's why you went to the trailer. He wanted to see you dressed Amish. You worked in the costume department and made the outfit. You told Nick it was totally authentic."

Kevin pushed her toward the car. "Let's go back to the studio. We can talk there."

She balked. "I'm not going anywhere with you."

"You're taking this too far, Becky." His tone hardened along with the glare in his eyes.

She jerked her hand from his hold. Snippets of conversation and flashes from the past played through her mind.

"You're wrong, Kevin." She steeled her gaze as she started to remember. "I didn't want anything to do with you or the movie business. I made the Amish costume and agreed to model it for the producer, but I had put in my notice and was leaving Montcliff Studio."

"You wanted to be a movie star."

She shook her head. "You wanted me in the film because you were tired of Vanessa and needed a new girlfriend, but I was never interested in you. Nor did I want to be a movie star."

"I'm tired of your foolishness." He grabbed her arm with one hand and shoved her forward. "You made me look like a fool to Mr. Walker."

"What about Vanessa Harrington, Kevin? You killed her. I went to Mr. Walker's office that night because you told me to. It was her blood on the rug."

He opened the van door and pushed Becca onto the passenger seat. She fought back. He fisted his hand and punched her stomach. She doubled over in the seat, the air whizzing from her lungs. She gasped, unable to breathe.

He lifted the bottom edge of his sweatshirt and pointed to the weapon stuck in his waistband. "Don't try to cross me, Becky."

Still struggling to breathe, she turned to glance at Mr. Gingerich's limp body. "Help…the old man," she gasped. "He's hurt…could freeze…to death."

"Which is exactly what I want." He slipped behind the wheel, turned the key, and the engine roared to life.

Despondent, she cowered away from him and

glanced back, seeing Mr. Gingerich. *Protect him, Lord. Send help.*

On the opposite side of the entrance road, movement caught her eye. Someone in a buggy. He jumped to the ground and ran toward the van just as it pulled out of the drive.

Zeke!

Once again, snow started to fall. Zeke ran all the faster, his arms reaching for her.

Kevin pushed down on the accelerator. The van fishtailed onto the road heading up the mountain.

She looked back, her heart breaking seeing Zeke as he continued to run after her.

Tears streamed down her face. She wasn't Amish, which meant she couldn't be with him. If she couldn't be with Zeke, nothing else mattered.

"Becca!" Zeke screamed as he ran after the van, his boots slipping in the snow. The van accelerated even more and disappeared around the bend.

The man who had chased Becca had found her.

Although frantic to save her, Zeke had to ensure Levi Gingerich was all right. He ran back to the older man, relieved to find him sitting up and wiping his head.

The cut on his forehead had stopped bleeding. Zeke put his hand under the man's shoulders. "Mr. Gingerich, let me take you someplace safe."

"Zeke, you've got to get that guy. Name's Kevin Adams. He claims to be a movie star. He wanted to find Caleb. He'll come back. You've got to warn my son."

"We can call him."

The old man shook his head. "My home phone's not working, and I refuse to get a cell."

Zeke sighed with frustration. "It is not safe for you to stay here, sir."

"It's my house. I'm not leaving."

"I'll take you to my aunt's house."

"You mean Hattie's place?"

"*Yah.* She will tend the cut on your forehead and give you something warm to eat."

Working quickly, Zeke eased Gingerich into the buggy and covered him with a blanket. Then he hurried Sophie down the hill. All the while, his heart was torn in two, thinking of Becca. Where had the guy taken her and what would he do to her?

Hattie heard their approach and was on the porch as they neared.

"What has happened?" she said, hurrying to help Levi down from the buggy.

Zeke filled her in. "Take care of Mr. Gingerich. I'll head up the mountain. I have to find Becca."

"Be careful, Zeke. The roads are icy."

"If Mike Frazier stops by, tell him I could use his help."

Once assured Levi and Hattie were safely inside with the doors locked, Zeke flicked the reins, encouraging Sophie onto the main road.

The low cloud cover and falling snow added to his concern about Becca, not knowing where she was and what the man planned to do with her.

"Giddyap, Sophie. We have to find, Becca."

Gray sunlight filtered through the dense clouds and barren trees. Glancing up, Zeke saw the waterfall in the distance. A flash of chrome from a vehicle appeared on the winding access road that led to the falls. His gut wrenched thinking of the boy who had fallen to his death, his body washed downstream and into the river, never to be found again.

"Gott," Zeke said, not knowing if his prayer would be heard. "Protect Becca and stop Kevin Adams. Forgive me for the mistakes in my past and let no harm come to Becca."

He clucked his tongue. Sophie increased her speed.

A fierce wind blew and the snow fell harder as they climbed in elevation. Zeke pulled his hat down farther on his head and blew into his hands to warm them. He had to get to the top of the mountain, but would he get there in time to save Becca?

TWENTY-THREE

Kevin was driving like a madman. Becca clutched the dash with one hand and the console with the other and gasped as they rounded each curve in the road. She looked out the passenger window at the sheer drop-off that rimmed the outside edge of the narrow roadway. Her stomach roiled, and she glanced away, unwilling to be frightened by the steep cliffs and river far below. She had enough to worry about with a crazed lunatic at the wheel.

"Slow down," she screamed. "You're going to kill us."

Kevin laughed. "That's the plan."

"What?"

"I'll make it look like you drove off the road. You took the van once you realized everyone knew you had killed Vanessa."

"I couldn't and wouldn't kill anyone."

"I'll tell people you wanted the lead role in the next movie. You made the Amish costume so Mr. Walker would give you the part. You had an Amish grandmother who taught you how to sew."

"So I truly am Amish." Relieved to confirm her ancestry, she was terrified of what might happened next.

"You lived with your grandparents more than a year, Becky, after your mother went to jail."

She wanted to cover her ears and drown out his voice. As much as she needed to remember her past, the fact that her mother was a criminal was too painful to bear.

"Once your grandparents died, you had no one. That's how you ended up working for the studio in the costume department. I was tired of Vanessa and wanted someone new. You weren't interested in me so I convinced Nick Walker to give you an acting role, hoping your feelings for me would soften."

"You tried to manipulate me, Kevin, but I wanted nothing to do with acting or with you."

"Vanessa got wind of my plan to convince Nick to give you an acting part. You know Vanessa. She had a temper and knew how to throw her weight around if someone tried to cross her."

Becca could see the carpet and the bloody weapon in her mind's eye. "You killed her, Kevin."

"I didn't kill her, but everything points to you being the killer."

"That's crazy."

"Maybe, except your fingerprints are on the letter opener."

"The letter opener with the Montcliff Studio logo on the shaft," she said, having a clearer vision of the murder weapon.

Kevin smiled. "You do remember."

"You killed Vanessa with the letter opener on the beige carpet with a lime green trellis design."

"Sounds like a kid's board game." He chuckled. "Vanessa tried to attack you."

"What?"

"She was in the office and overheard me and Nick talking about giving you a part in the next film. Vanessa thought Nick was going to give you *her* part. You stepped inside, never realizing Vanessa was there. She grabbed a marble statue off the bookcase and knocked you out. Then she found the letter opener and raised it to strike you."

Becca shivered. "But you killed her first."

"Actually, the producer killed her in self-defense. Vanessa turned on him. She knew Nick was no longer willing to put up with her tantrums."

"The sheriff will arrest both of you."

"We wiped the letter opener clean and then placed it in your hands so your fingerprints would be on it."

"Then you tried to clean the bloodstained carpet with bleach."

"I grabbed the wrong product. Instead of removing the bloodstain, it removed all the color. That's why we threw the rug over the ledge where you had fallen. I tried to catch up to you that night and saw you slip and fall. I thought you had died."

"No wonder you looked surprised when you saw me in town."

"You mean at the Cattle Auction?"

"You were the Amish man who chased me."

He nodded. "I was in costume for the filming of the trailer for the next movie. I had seen you walking along the road that first day and chased you into the pasture. Once I realized you were alive. I kept trying to find you. After Nick got back to the studio, we decided to make it look like you committed the murder. We were on the ledge soon after you and that Amish guy must have found the carpet."

"A rug won't prove I killed anyone."

"No, but the murder weapon will. We took the small quilt from your bedroom at the studio and wrapped the letter opener in it."

The green patched quilt she had made with her grandmother.

"The weapon bears your prints, Becky, which will prove you murdered Vanessa. The motive is clear. You wanted Vanessa's part in the next movie. We've thought of everything."

"What if Nick accuses you of being the killer?" she posed, hoping to burst his euphoria.

Kevin snickered, like a child, and patted his shirt pocket. "I videotaped Nick with my phone. He was in a rage and stabbed Vanessa over and over. He never saw me, but the video is proof in case he shifts the blame to me."

Knowing she was running out of time, Becca scooted closer to the door. As they rounded a curve, a gust of wind hit the van. Kevin struggled to keep the vehicle on the road.

Becca raised her leg and jammed her foot into Kevin's injured thigh where she had stabbed him with the pitchfork.

He groaned and lost control of the wheel. The car skidded across the icy roadway.

She screamed, fearing they would plummet over the edge.

Just in time, he turned the wheel toward the mountain. The van went into another skid.

Her heart stopped.

A giant boulder came up to greet them as they crashed into the side of the mountain.

Becca's head slammed against the dashboard. She moaned and glanced at the gauge on the console. Someone had inactivated both airbags.

Kevin lay slumped over the steering wheel.

She groped for the knob and pushed open the door. She had to get away.

The wind whipped around her head, tearing at her bonnet and sending it flying. Her outer cape billowed as the wind caught in its folds. She slipped and slid down the incline, needing to escape the man who had run after her that night in the woods.

She tripped. Her hands caught her fall, the ice on the roadway as cold as her chilling fear. She stumbled to her feet and continued on.

The car door opened. Footsteps sounded behind her.

"No," she screamed. Kevin grabbed her and threw her to the ground.

"You can't run from me, Becky. I've got to teach you a lesson. People will be upset when they learn you killed Vanessa and tossed her over the ledge. They'll also be upset when they find your body at the bottom of the waterfall. Or maybe they'll never find you."

"Kevin, please. I didn't do anything to hurt you."

"That's not true. You rejected me. You weren't interested in what I offered you. Sometimes I can't keep things straight, but I know one thing. You rejected me so you need to die."

Zeke saw the studio van that had crashed into a boulder on the side of the mountain. His breath caught in his throat.

Where is she? Where is Becca?

Peering down from the buggy, he looked through the open van door to the empty interior and flicked the reins. Sophie forged on. Her pace slow but steady as she labored along the narrow roadway.

Rounding the next bend, Zeke's heart stopped. He recognized the movie star from the photo Caleb had shown him. Kevin was standing near the top of the ledge, holding a gun to Becca's head.

Behind him, water spewed over the falls. Ice had formed on the edge of the rock, making it all appear surreal.

"Let her go." Zeke pulled back on the reins. "She has done nothing wrong."

Kevin laughed. "She rejected me to sew costumes. She wasn't even interested when I offered her a part in the next movie."

Fear flashed from Becca's eyes.

Zeke raised his voice over the roar of the falling water. "Take me as your hostage instead of her."

The man sneered. "Don't be a fool, Amish. Both of you are my hostages. Bring your buggy closer to the edge."

"Becca, move toward the mountain and away from the ledge." Zeke's voice was firm.

Kevin pushed her aside. "Do what he says, Becky. You'll be with your Amish boyfriend soon enough."

He motioned Zeke forward. "Bring the buggy closer."

Sophie pinned her ears back. She pawed the snow.

"Go on, girl," Zeke encouraged under his breath. "We will show this city slicker how smart you are."

Zeke encouraged her closer.

The movie star grabbed the harness. "Nice horse."

"Easy, Sophie," Zeke soothed.

Kevin pulled his phone from his pocket and motioned to Becca. "Get in the buggy with your boyfriend. I want to take your picture."

She shook her head. "I'm not moving."

"Do what I say, Becky. Now."

A car sounded behind them. Zeke let out a breath of relief and turned to welcome the new arrival, expecting to see Mike Frazier or one of the other sheriff's deputies. His gut tightened when he saw the Montcliff Studio logo on the side of the van.

Nick Walker, the producer, climbed from the vehicle, gun in hand. "What's going on, Kevin?"

"Just getting rid of our murderer and her boyfriend."

Nick pointed to Zeke. "Why'd you include him?"

"We'll say they were working together. It only makes our story better. We found Becky and tried to talk her into giving herself up, but she and her boyfriend headed to the waterfall. We'll call it Lover's Leap, just like in the movies. They couldn't face going to jail and a future without one another."

The producer scowled. "You're a fool, Kevin."

"What?" Anger flashed from the leading man's eyes. "I'm the one who stayed behind to clean up the mess you made."

"And ruined the carpet."

"I got rid of the rug and recarpeted the entryway. That kid from food services is our only problem."

Nick laughed. "I took care of Landers and the kid from food services won't make it down the mountain. I tampered with his car. Both of them knew too much. Their deaths are unfortunate but will not be tied to either of us." He pointed to Becca and Zeke. "Now we need to get rid of these two."

Zeke had expected law enforcement to come to their aid. Time was running out. Zeke could not rely on the sheriff or his men. He had to find a way to save Becca, even if it cost him his life.

TWENTY-FOUR

Chilled to the core, Becca rubbed her hands over her arms and tried to think. She had to do something, but what?

Nick Walker glared at her.

"You killed Vanessa," she stated, hoping to throw him off guard.

He narrowed his gaze.

"You killed her," she continued. "Kevin told me."

Nick laughed nervously and glanced at the leading man. "You talk too much."

"We'll take care of them, Nick. I promise."

"You can't do anything right." The producer grabbed Becca's arm and shoved her toward the buggy.

"No!" She tried to jerk free.

Zeke leaped down to protect her.

The producer jammed his gun against her head. "Stay back, Mr. Amish, or she dies."

"Let her go," Zeke demanded, his hands fisted.

The producer laughed. "I thought the Amish were nonviolent. Read my lips. You breathe, and she dies."

He dragged Becca to the buggy still holding the gun

against her temple. "Get in. Now. Or I'll kill your boy-friend."

"You'll kill him anyway."

Kevin stood in front of the mare and jerked forward on the harness. "Come on. Nice horse."

"Back," Zeke commanded under his breath.

Sophie pinned her ears. She whooshed her tail and took a step back.

Nick twisted Becca's right arm behind her. "Climb in. Now."

Her left hand was numb from the cold as she tried to grab the metal arm rail. She raised her foot, but her shoe slipped on the icy step and she fell against Sophie's flank.

The mare reared up. Her front hooves nearly hit Kevin. He dropped the harness and jumped back. His feet slipped. He tried to right himself and flailed his arms. Zeke lunged around the buggy and reached for him, but not in time.

Kevin's eyes widened. His splayed fingers clawed at the icy ledge, unable to grab hold.

"No!" he screamed as he slipped over the edge.

Becca gasped and covered her mouth with her hand, fearing she would be sick.

Zeke seized the reins and backed Sophie away from the ledge. "Good, girl. Easy now."

The producer sneered. "I planned to kill Kevin. You saved me the trouble. We'll forget the buggy. Both of you can jump off the ledge. Kevin was right. We'll call this Lover's Leap."

Unable to comprehend his callous disregard for life, Becca moved toward him. Out of the corner of her eye, she saw Zeke rounding the far side of the buggy.

"You're evil," she shouted at the producer, flailing her arms as a distraction. "You killed Vanessa and Larry Landers and now you caused another person to die, but you won't get away with any of the crimes."

He laughed. "You're amusing, Becky, and much too righteous, especially since the police will learn you killed Vanessa as well as Kevin."

She took another step toward him. "Do you know what *righteousness* means, Mr. Walker?" She accentuated his name as if he were scum. "It means God-fearing and virtuous. A righteous person is decent and honorable, not like you."

"My, my, you might have an acting ability after all. What a shame you won't star in our next movie. Now get back with your Amish boyfriend."

He glanced toward the buggy and hesitated for half a second. Long enough for Zeke, who had inched around the rear of the buggy, to tackle him. The producer crashed to the icy ground with a thud. The gun flew from his hand.

A siren sounded. Zeke turned as Mike Frazier pulled his cruiser to a stop. The deputy jumped from the sedan, gun raised and at the ready.

Zeke quickly filled him in.

Mike cuffed the producer, read him his Miranda rights and then shoved him into the rear of his squad car. He secured the producer's weapon while Becca explained what Kevin Adams had revealed.

"Nicholas Walker killed Vanessa," she said. "They wiped the letter opener clean and put it in my hand so my prints would be on the shaft. Kevin tried to clean the rug and then threw it over the ledge."

"Our guys found the rug about an hour ago. They

used bleach on the main stain, but blood spatter was also found on other areas of the rug. We'll have the forensic guys check it out."

"Kevin's phone," Becca suddenly remembered. "He made a video that shows the producer stabbing Vanessa."

Mike Frazier glanced around. "So where's the actor and his phone?"

Zeke peered over the edge. "Lying on a ledge about twenty feet down. I have rope in the back of the buggy."

"You'd be crazy to go down the mountain in this weather," Mike said.

Zeke looked at the deputy and smiled. "Like old times, Mike, when we were kids."

"Don't do it," Becca pleaded. "It's too dangerous."

"The storm will only get worse. The wind's increasing. Our only chance to save Kevin is for me to go down now."

Zeke guided Sophie into a turn so the mare and the buggy were faced away from the cliff. He gave the reins to Becca, and then tossed his hat into the buggy and slipped on his heavy work gloves.

"Give me a hand, Mike. We did this when we were kids. We can do it again today. I can make a Swiss seat out of extra rope and use snaplinks to secure Kevin so we can haul him up."

Mike nodded. "It's worth a try, if you're willing to take the risk."

Working quickly, they anchored two ropes to the buggy. Mike helped Zeke thread another rope between his legs and around his waist to make a seat. Together they attached the rappelling ropes to the seat with a snaplink.

Once satisfied with the position of the ropes, Mike nodded.

Zeke glanced at Becca, then walked backward. He crouched low and disappeared over the edge.

Her heart nearly stopped, and she trembled, not only from cold but also from fear.

Gott, help Zeke. Protect him, she prayed silently.

She stood next to the buggy, holding Sophie's reins. "Steady, girl."

"He made it to the lower ledge," Mike shouted back to her.

"I found something else," Zeke called, his voice barely audible over the howling wind and the waterfall.

After what seemed like an eternity, she heard his voice again.

"Pull up."

"Let's go, Sophie," Becca said to the mare. "Come on, girl. Nice and slow."

Sophie shook her mane then took a step forward, then another and another.

The deputy worked the rope at the edge of the ledge.

Kevin's man bun came into view. Mike grabbed his shoulder and the rope that secured his arms and pulled him over the edge. The movie star appeared unconscious but still alive. Mike disconnected the ropes and threw them back to Zeke.

Becca held her breath.

"Pull." Zeke's voice.

She encouraged Sophie forward.

A face appeared, then a man's body.

Zeke!

Relief swept over her, and she blinked back tears of joy.

* * *

"He needs medical attention," Zeke shouted over the wind after assessing Kevin's injury. "We must get him down the mountain." Working quickly, Zeke and the deputy bundled the movie star into the squad car.

Zeke handed the deputy the cell phone. "This is what I also found on the ledge. Play the video, Mike. You will find out the truth about Vanessa Harrington's murder."

"I need the judge to okay a warrant, Zeke. Besides, it's too cold for a cell phone to work out here."

"The producer mentioned tampering with Caleb Gingerich's car. Do you know anything about him?"

Mike nodded. "His car was stalled on the side of the mountain. One of my deputies picked him up, along with his father from your aunt's house. Both of them were taken to the hospital for evaluation. As far as I know, they're both doing well."

Zeke nodded his thanks, then headed to his buggy.

Becca sat wrapped in blankets in the front seat, waiting for Zeke.

"You should go with the deputy," he said as he climbed in next to her. "His squad car has a heater."

She shook her head. "I'll stay with you."

Mike Frazier waved as he started down the mountain. Zeke flicked the reins and encouraged Sophie. More than anything, he wanted to pull Becca into his arms and hold her close, yet she looked tired and cold and probably still in shock after everything that had happened.

The initial blow to her head had been severe enough to block her memory. He feared more damage had been done today. When he glanced at her pretty face, his gut twisted, seeing the new bruises and scrapes, feeling responsible. If only he had worked harder to keep her safe.

"Thank you for all you did, Zeke," she said, her voice little more than a whisper. "I never wanted to be a bother."

He smiled weakly. "You bring joy to my life, Becca. You could never be a bother."

She rubbed her forehead. "I still don't remember everything from my past."

"Whatever happened in the past remains there. Today starts now. Who you are is who you are at this moment." He took her hand. "Much has happened today. You need some of Hattie's good cooking and a sound night's sleep. Tomorrow will be a new day."

As usual, Hattie saw them coming and stepped onto the porch as the buggy came to a stop.

"Oh, Becca, it is so good to see you. Come, dear, you need to sit near the stove. There's coffee and a pot of hot soup to warm you."

Zeke helped Becca down from the buggy. She was so light in his arms. He wanted to hold on to her forever and never let her go.

She glanced up at him questioningly.

"Go inside and get warm," he encouraged. "I'll take care of Sophie."

"Give her an extra treat for working so hard to get us down the mountain."

Zeke nodded, grateful to have heard the first spark of lightness in Becca's tone.

"Oh, Hattie." Becca glanced down at the green dress, as if seeing the smudged dirt and tears in the fabric for the first time today. "Look what I have done to this beautiful dress."

Hattie rubbed her hand over Becca's shoulder as if to

soothe her worry. "We can always make more dresses, dear, as long as you are with us."

Becca smiled and followed Hattie into the house.

Zeke looked at the falling snow, feeling cold and alone and fearful of what Becca would decide to do with her life.

She was *Englisch*.

Amish men only marry Amish women. Zeke had some soul-searching to do tonight.

After feeding Sophie and ensuring the mare was warm and dry, he hurried inside. Becca had gone upstairs, claiming she was too exhausted to eat.

He missed her already. What would he do if she left him for good? The thought cut to his heart.

TWENTY-FIVE

Zeke sat by the woodstove in the rocking chair after Hattie had gone to bed, reading from her Bible. The house was quiet, the only sound the crackling fire. Using the end iron, he rearranged the burning wood and threw another log into the stove, watching as the bright embers danced around the flames.

He shut the cast-iron load door and settled back in the rocker, turning again to Hattie's Bible, the worn pages bringing comfort.

Glancing up, he saw Becca standing in the open entryway to the kitchen. He placed the Bible on the side table and stood. "I did not hear you come downstairs."

"Hattie told me you were still up."

Becca's hair hung free around her shoulders. Her green eyes were filled with question.

"Hattie also told me that which I'm searching for may be right before me." She stepped closer.

"Decisions take time, Becca. Do not rush yourself."

"I wanted to know about my past so I would understand my future, but what I found confused me more."

"Your past is not important."

"Perhaps not, but you still need to know some of

what I've remembered. I was born in Birmingham and my grandparents came from Ethridge, Tennessee."

"An Amish community is located there."

She straightened her spine and pulled in a deep breath. "I never knew my father. My mother was imprisoned in Montgomery for a drug offense and released last year."

"What about you, Becca?"

"I've held a number of jobs—waitress, supermarket cashier, retail clerk—before I took the seamstress job with Montcliff. When I put in my notice to leave the studio, my supervisor said she was pleased with my work and was ready to increase my pay."

"Then you plan to stay?"

"Not at Montcliff. Hattie said she enjoys my presence here."

He stepped closer. "There is someone else who enjoys your presence and everything else about you."

She tilted her head.

"You don't know much about me, Zeke."

"I know how you make me feel, Becca." He touched her hair and ran his fingers down her cheek. The confusion he had read earlier in her green eyes softened.

"I want to talk to your father."

He waited, not knowing what she else would say.

"I need to know if his district would welcome me."

"You wish to be baptized?" he asked.

She nodded. "Why would I look elsewhere when everything I've ever wanted is right in front of me?"

He smiled, his heart nearly bursting with joy. "I plan to talk to my *datt*, as well."

"Baptism?" she asked.

He nodded.

She touched her hand to his chest. "You will bring joy to your father's heart."

"And to my own. My only hesitation was not knowing what you would do."

"And now you know. Does that change anything?"

"It only makes me a very happy man." He gazed into her eyes and found them filled with longing. "If we are both to be Amish, we will have time for courting. Perhaps you would allow me to take you on a buggy ride?"

She laughed. "Only if you promise no trips to Lover's Leap. I want to stay away from waterfalls and icy roads."

"But Amish Mountain? You could live there?"

"*Yah*, I will stay with Hattie for now if her invitation stands."

He took her hand. "That is the near future, Becca, but I am looking far ahead."

She stepped closer. "What do you see?"

"I see my life as an Amish farmer, with children to bring laughter to my home, land to work, a faith to sustain me. Most important, I see a beautiful woman to walk with me into the future."

"Tell me more about the woman you see."

He touched her cheek and trailed his fingers around her neck. "I see chestnut hair and green eyes, high cheekbones and full lips that are meant for kissing."

"Are you sure?"

He nodded, then lowered his lips to hers. All the love that filled his heart burst forth like the bright embers in the fire.

He pulled her closer and kissed her again, deeply, and again and again, never wanting anything to pull them apart.

Finally, she eased back. Her lips were swollen, her eyes soft and inviting, her cheeks flushed.

"I love you, Becca Troyer or Becky Taylor."

"You're sure?"

"Cross my heart."

Then he pulled her deeper into his embrace and continued to kiss her. The fire crackled and warmed the house all the while the snow fell outside and covered the world with a blanket of white. No matter what would come in the future, they would always be secure with *Gott*'s love and their love for one another.

"Marry me, Becca. I want to be with you for as long as *Gott* gives us."

"Oh, Zeke, that's what I want. To be with you always. The past is over and the only thing that matters is today and tomorrow and what we make of the future."

"A future together," he whispered before he kissed her again.

EPILOGUE

Sunshine poured through the bedroom window as Becca finished whipping the hem on the wedding dress, pleased with the blue-green fabric she and Hattie had found in town.

"It accents your eyes," Hattie had said, then insisted on paying for the material. "Plus, the wedding will be held at my house. It is the least I can do. You and Zeke have brought much joy to my life."

Warmed by Hattie's generosity, Becca held the dress up and smiled with approval at her own workmanship. Not taking pride but appreciating all her grandmother had taught her. She thought again of her loving *mammi* who had been that source of refuge in Becca's early life.

Over the last few months, her memory had slowly returned with a clear picture of the dysfunction that had surrounded her early years. Some memories had been hard to accept, yet with Hattie's and Zeke's help and with prayer, she had come to understand her wayward mother better and had forgiven her for the havoc she had created in Becca's younger days. If not for the firm foundation provided by her Amish grandparents, Becca's life would have turned out so differently.

"I am grateful," she said aloud, thinking of how the Lord had protected her and brought her to Amish Mountain. She hoped someday she and her mother would reconnect, if it was *Gott*'s will.

Stepping to the window, she saw Zeke hauling lumber toward the new house next door. As if sensing her gaze, he glanced up and smiled. She waved, her heart nearly bursting with gladness.

She hung the dress on the wall peg and hurried downstairs. The smell of fresh baked pastry filled the house with an aroma that made her mouth water.

"I finished the wedding dress," she announced as she entered the kitchen. Hattie pulled a pie from the oven, and Becca raced to place the cooling rack on the counter.

"Zeke and I can never thank you enough, Hattie, for all you've done and for insisting we have the wedding here."

"It gives me a reason to cook, *yah*? Less than a week away, and there is much to do. So many people will be here. Old friends, relatives. Everyone wants to take part in the celebration." Her eyes twinkled. "But I like a full house. Zeke's father is coming for lunch today. You can talk more about the wedding with him. I invited Annie Shrock."

"The widow who hosted the quilting I attended?"

"*Yah*. Her husband died last year. She is lonely. So is Zeke's father. He has mourned for my sister too long."

"And what about you, Hattie? Levi Gingerich seems to be stopping by more often these days since he asked forgiveness and returned to the faith."

Hattie blushed and turned back to the stove. "We

were friends in our youth. I am glad to have him as a friend again."

"He seems like a new man."

Hattie nodded. "Thanks to Caleb's insistence that he go to a cardiologist. The medicine for his heart helped. He feels better and is able to do more."

"He is also happy about the way Zeke and Caleb repaired his home and the fences on his farm."

"*Yah*, and Caleb is helping him more and more. The young man remains *Englisch*, but we will see what the future will hold. At least he got rid of his sports car."

The future. Becca smiled, thinking of sharing her life with Zeke. "Do you need any help, Hattie?"

The woman made a shooing motion. "The midday meal is almost ready. Tell Zeke his father will be here soon."

Becca hugged Hattie, then raced outside to where Zeke was sanding a piece of wood. She stopped a few steps away to once again take in the house that would be their new home after the wedding.

Sensing her presence, he turned, dropped the sandpaper and opened his arms. She ran into his embrace, smelling the fresh cut wood and newly plowed Georgia soil in the distance.

"I did not know my future husband would be such an accomplished carpenter. You can do everything, Zeke. I have heard the townspeople talk. You climb mountains, you turn struggling acreage into a productive farm. You help your neighbors and have brought joy back to your father's heart. They also talk about how you and your dad worked with the new producer at Montcliff to ensure the studio provides wholesome films and a good working environment for its employees."

"Are you listening to town gossip, Becca?" His lips twitched playfully.

"I listen only to the truth, Ezekiel Hochstetler."

"Soon my time will be taken up with other endeavors," he teased.

She raised a brow. "What are you talking about?"

He winked. "A new husband must ensure his wife is well loved."

Her cheeks warmed and her heart skittered in her chest. "You are making me blush. What would your father say?"

"He would encourage me all the more. As he told me after church last Sunday, he is eager for grandchildren."

She snuggled into his arms. "Children will come in *Gott*'s perfect time. You told me to take each day as it comes, although I must admit our wedding cannot come soon enough."

"Another few days," he said. "The house will be finished just in time."

"Do Amish husbands carry their new brides over the threshold as the *Englisch* do?"

He laughed. "If this is something you want, I would be happy to carry you anywhere."

"The only place I want to be is with you, Zeke. As confused as my early life was, everything worked together to bring me to Amish Mountain. Looking back, I am able to accept my past because I know *Gott* was leading me to you and to this moment."

He looked down at her, his eyes filled with love that she knew would last forever. "And you are the reason I returned to the mountain, Becca. I knew in my deepest core that I would find you someday. You told me I had built a wall around my heart. You were right. You broke down that wall and saved me from becoming a bitter man. I was dying, but you brought me back to life."

"Just as you and Hattie gave me shelter and saved me when I didn't even know my name."

"We no longer need to look back, Becca, but only enjoy today and tomorrow and all the days ahead."

He gazed for a long moment into her eyes. The world stood still, and all she could see was the righteous man she loved. Then ever so slowly, he lowered his lips to hers.

A weaker woman would have died from the burst of love that exploded in her heart, but Becca had been strengthened by adversity and was strong in her commitment to make a wonderful life for her soon-to-be husband and the children *Gott* would provide.

Then she stopped thinking of anything except the warmth of Zeke's embrace and his kisses that, she knew, would continue to thrill her for the rest of her life.

* * * * *

If you enjoyed this story look for these other books by Debby Giusti:

Amish Rescue
Amish Christmas Secrets
Amish Safe House

Dear Reader,

I hope you enjoyed *Her Forgotten Amish Past*. When reclusive farmer Ezekiel Hochstetler finds a battered woman in an Amish dress wandering on a dark mountain road late at night, his peaceful world turns upside down. The fact that she doesn't know her name or anything about her past adds to his confusion. The last thing Becca Troyer remembers is being chased through the dark woods. Untying her past puts Zeke and Becca in danger not only of losing their hearts but also their lives.

I pray for my readers each day and would love to hear from you. Email me at debby@debbygiusti.com or write me c/o Love Inspired, 195 Broadway, 24th Floor, New York, NY 10007. Visit me at www.debbygiusti.com and at www.Facebook.com/debby.giusti.9.

As always, I thank God for bringing us together through this story.

Wishing you abundant blessings,

Debby Giusti

Get 4 FREE REWARDS!

We'll send you 2 FREE Books plus 2 FREE Mystery Gifts.

Love Inspired® Suspense books feature Christian characters facing challenges to their faith... and lives.

FREE Value Over $20

SPECIAL EXCERPT FROM

Love Inspired
SUSPENSE

*When a police detective stumbles upon a murder scene
with no body, can the secret father of her child help her
solve the case without becoming the next victim?*

Read on for a sneak preview of
Holiday Homecoming Secrets *by Lynette Eason,
available December 2019 from Love Inspired Suspense.*

Bryce Kingsley bolted toward the opening of the deserted mill and stepped inside, keeping one hand on the weapon at his side. "Jade?"

"Back here." Her voice reached him, sounding weak, shaky.

He hurried to her, keeping an eye on the surrounding area. Bryce rounded the end of the spindle row to see Jade on the floor, holding her head. Blood smeared a short path down her cheek. "You're hurt!" For a moment, she simply stared up at him, complete shock written across her features. "Jade? Hello?"

She blinked. "Bryce?"

"Hi." He glanced over his shoulder, then swung the beam of the flashlight over the rest of the interior.

"You're here?"

"Yeah. This wasn't exactly the way I wanted to let you know I was coming home, but—"

"What are you doing here?"

"Can we discuss that later? Let's focus on you and the fact you're bleeding from a head wound."

"I…I'm all right."

"Did you get a look at who hit you?"

"No."

A car door slammed. Blue lights whirled through the broken windows and bounced off the concrete-and-brick walls. Bryce helped her to her feet. "Let's get that head looked at."

"Wait." He could see her pulling herself together, the shock of his appearance fading. "I need to take a look at something."

He frowned. "Okay." She went to the old trunk next to the wall. "What is it?"

"The person who hit me was very interested in whatever was over here."

Bryce nodded to the shovel and disturbed dirt in front of the trunk. "Looks like he was trying to dig something up."

"What does this look like to you?"

"Looks like someone's been digging."

"Yes, but why? What could they possibly be looking for out here?"

"Who knows?" Bryce studied the pile of dirt and the bricks. "Actually, I don't think they were looking for anything. I think they were in the middle of *burying* something."

Don't miss
Holiday Homecoming Secrets *by Lynette Eason,*
available December 2019 wherever
Love Inspired® Suspense books and ebooks are sold.

LoveInspired.com

LISEXP1119

Discover wholesome and uplifting stories of faith, forgiveness and hope.

Join our social communities to connect with other readers who share your love!

Sign up for the Love Inspired newsletter at **LoveInspired.com** to be the first to find out about upcoming titles, special promotions and exclusive content.

CONNECT WITH US AT:

Facebook.com/groups/HarlequinConnection

 Facebook.com/LoveInspiredBooks

 Twitter.com/LoveInspiredBks

LISOCIAL2019